Blue Mirage

STAR

ISBN: 9780984041633
Published by: Johnson Publications
Newtown Square PA

Cover layout/design by Designs by SheShe
Editors: Carla Dean U Can Mark My Word Editing

Printed in the United States of America

Contact for comments or to order books:
www.johnsonpublications.biz

Dedication

To my two loving sons. You are the reason I strive to reach the stars, so that even if I miss them, I will have made them a little closer in your view. You both are my lifeline. Thank you for showing me life at its best.

Thank You

I thank GOD for giving me the ability to express myself freely.

When I say thank you, I mean it from my heart to those who love me and those who appreciate my craft. Without my readers, I would have no reason to write. I love you all for your support.

To my husband, my partner, and my friend–Thank you for always lifting me up and holding my hand through celebration and sorrow. I Love You!

To my mother–Thank you for teaching me that the sky is the limit to what I can have. You are my rock. I Love You! To my brother and sister– I love you both. Thank you for all of the support!

Thank you to all of my other family and friends. There is strength in numbers, and from you, I draw the strength that I need when the world seems to be too harsh.

Special thanks to Antonia Adolphues. You pulled this off! You are definitely destined for greatness. Your professionalism on this project was that of an accomplished writer. Reach for your dreams and you just might get them.

Blue Mirage

Intro...

Screams echoed off the cement walls. As Shanna clawed at the bricks, her hands slipped from the moisture. She trembled with fear while gagging from the strong smell of dogs.

"Help! Help!" she yelled.

All she heard was the pounding of fading footsteps and the jingling of keys. She tried to run away, but the confined space made it impossible. As she looked down, the K-9 dogs barked at her feet while the sound of dripping water disturbed her.

"Stop! Help! I did not do it!" she yelled.

Thump! Shanna hit the floor, and her eyes grew wide. Her body shook uncontrollably as she sat straight up.

"Oh shit! I almost got eaten by the dog that time."

She was shaken, but happy to know it wasn't real. It was just another nightmare about the awful things she had been through. Despite the nightmares and thoughts about her life moving forward, she had to start her day.

Shanna awoke to the sound of rain hitting her window. She thought about what her day would bring. She had so much to sort out, so much to do. Things had not been the same since…that day.

While shuffling things around on her desk, Shanna came across a big envelope that she had put off opening for a few days. She reluctantly opened it, and its contents were nothing short of disturbing.

Everything that happened came back to her mind as she franticly searched through the unmarked package. Shanna rummaged through her desk to find a pen. She had to document the package's arrival in her journal...

Time: 9:30 a.m.

Place: Home office; sitting at the window

Mood: SHOCKED

I will start by saying that this is a very complicated story to tell. I have never been so confused in my life about the roles that authority figures play in the place that I work. I am relieved to write this, but at the same time, I feel a profound sense of sadness and disappointment. The people involved in my story are deceitful, and they need to pay for their actions. The past year of my life has been nothing short of colorful. They create a mirage that fools all that they come in contact with. A mirage, by definition, is an optical illusion caused by an atmospheric condition. That is exactly what happened in this situation. Beware: you will hear some things that will shock you, but pay close attention so as not to get caught up in THE BLUE MIRAGE. Accompanying this journal entry are

3

pictures, audiotapes, and a manuscript to support this story.

Signed,

S.B.

Chapter 1

IT ALL STARTED WHEN...

T he day seemed to be going well for Diashana Butler, known as Shanna for short. The sun was shining, and she felt well rested after her midnight escapade with the love of her life, Tristen Stevens.

Tristen enhanced her status or rather they complemented each other. Tristen had the privilege to rub elbows with the upper class, which afforded him opportunities that would set them both up for life. Shanna was no slouch, either. She was blessed with brains and beauty, but always remained down to earth. This attribute is what Tristen loved most about her. With her on his team and keeping him grounded, he would be seen as the people's mayor. Her job at the prison, while not prominent to most, allowed her to live a certain lifestyle. She was the head of her department and had a starting salary of sixty thousand dollars.

Shanna was a sensual-looking female, and she pulled that off without trying. She always looked as if she was seducing any man in her view, which caused many women that she met to hold on tight to their men. She had a medium build and hips that were perfectly proportioned with her ass and thighs. Her face was smooth as milk chocolate and the home of two chestnut brown eyes with long, jet-black lashes that she used to flutter regularly.

The only child and her parents' pride and joy, Shanna was a 32-year-old female who had done all right for herself. She was the Director of Inmate Programs at Pinckney Peabody Correctional Facility in Philadelphia, Pennsylvania.

Shanna entered the prison and walked straight to the sign-in desk just as she had done for the past five years. The ritual was familiar, but not this particular morning. As the last letter of her name hit the page, she felt a swift gust of wind. When she looked up, she could not believe her eyes. Surrounded by men and women wearing all black uniforms, she was escorted to the captain's office.

The fifty-foot walk seemed like ten miles. Shanna's breathing quickened, and she could feel the blood thicken in her veins. She questioned the officers' reason for the dramatic entrance, but none of the glorified correctional officers spoke a word. Once she was placed in the office, the lieutenant appeared, seeming agitated. Without introduction, he ordered her to tell them whom she was smuggling in drugs for. Shanna was definitely no angel, but far from a drug pusher. She attempted to wake up from this nightmare, but to no avail. The lieutenant's rotten breath and loud screams confirmed she was definitely awake. He spouted names at her while producing his angriest snarl.

After getting her thoughts together, Shanna said, "What the hell are you talking about? I want to see my lawyer!"

The captain smiled and replied, "This is the PPS. In here, you do what you are told! And right now, you're going to get strip-searched. Then your locker and vehicle will be searched, also, as stated in the PPS search policy: (a)1234."

Shanna reared back in her seat and looked at the captain, the lieutenant, and the burly, wide-eyed female sergeant.

"Who in the hell do you think you're fucking with?" she yelled.

"If you have nothing to hide, we wouldn't be having this conversation," the captain replied. "Now, follow the sergeant's orders and drop 'em. I'll be outside."

Captain John Stern was a tall white man in his mid forties, one of the few Anglo-Saxons left that thought he was pure bred. So, the thought of an educated black was almost impossible to him, which was his reasoning for choosing corrections as his career. Captain Stern made it up the ranks, kicking ass all the way. He did not care who he hurt in the process, as long as he was glorified in the end. The straightforward, follow-the-orders mentality and a chain of command suited him. He got off on power, especially power over women and other minorities. His drawers were in a bunch since his new warden's first day and his old Academy buddy's departure. His new boss was black *and* female, which made her twice as repulsive. The thought that she may have fucked her way to the top bugged him even more.

Shanna sat back in the hard wooden chair that reminded her of her grade school days and started to reminisce about several events in the prison. She strolled her cortex to recall a series of events that led up to that point in her life. Her life flashed before her like a movie in slow motion. She could smell the pungent aroma of the K-9 unit, which further confirmed it was her reality. She escaped from her body and became numb. All activity around her was nothing but background noise. As she sat there with tears flowing down her face like rushing water in the Caribbean, it all made sense...

Chapter 2

The halls were packed for miles; the only things visible were men in brown jumpsuits. They came in all different hues and sizes. Shanna made her way through the crowd as four officers escorted the inmates to the gym and to afternoon activities at Peabody Corrections. Shanna entered the activity room and, as usual, the room was not set up for her creative writing class. The chairs were stacked on top of each other, and the room smelled like hot, sweaty ass. There were no supplies for the day's lesson, and there was no officer willing to assist her with bringing the inmates to the class.

That was nothing new to deal with in the prison system. Most of the people who worked there hated their job or were too lazy to actually do their job. The other group hated the inmates and treated them like shit on a stick. But, not Shanna. She was compassionate and treated them like human beings. She never in a million years thought such animals would employ her. Her career path was law, but she never pursued it after she lost the state finals mock trial in high school. After the loss her debate team endured, she felt unworthy of practicing law.

Shanna took the chairs and placed them in a classroom formation. The room was an institutionalized cream color with cement walls. The large window on the left wall allowed for some visibility of the outside world.

The inmates came streaming into the room, laughing and playing among each other like children. Shanna's personality was no-holds-barred, so she said whatever she felt.

"Come into my classroom and stop acting like confused puppies fresh out the womb!"

They just stared at her. They were used to her abrasive comments; they knew she meant nothing by them.

"Ms. Butler, did you miss me?" a voice yelled over the noise in the room.

"Yeah, I missed you like I miss cramps!" she replied, causing the entire class to laugh out loud.

"Damn, Ms. Butler! You must be in your bag today."

"Nigga, I'm in my bag, and I'm about to put you in it, too, if you don't shut the hell up and let me start the damn class!"

Shanna started her class as she always did. The men went around the room talking about what they were upset about or happy about. The back and forth joking and word play went on throughout the remainder of the class. Despite the horseplay, Shanna actually reached some of the inmates and had them thinking about becoming serious with writing after they were released.

Shanna could see the lieutenant's office from her classroom. He didn't like staff being respectful of the inmates. He had a suspicious nature that came from him working in internal affairs for fifteen years. Lieutenant Greenwich was a medium built Caucasian man that looked to be in his early forties, but was really in his fifties. He had a few secrets of his own, with the major one being that he craved Black women.

He stared at Shanna's plump ass each time she walked by him. That day was no different. Shanna wore a black blazer and some True Religion stretch jeans that grabbed her body at each curve. The lieutenant eyed her the entire morning, but not for the reasons that Shanna believed. The lieutenant got off on watching her and often fantasized about how soft her body would feel against his; but today was business. His phone rang.

"Lieutenant Greenwich here!"

A female's voice on the other end greeted him. "Are you free to talk?"

"Who is this?"

"You know I don't tell my name on the phone. I just need to know are you working on that project."

"Yes, it is under surveillance right now. I won't know anything for a few days. I will call you then."

The class was over, and Shanna appeared in the lieutenant's doorway. He looked up, and startled, he abruptly hung up the phone.

"May I help you with something, Ms. Butler?"

"Sure. You can lock the room back up. I'm on my way out."

He sat there looking straight through her. "Okay, I will handle it," he said.

As he watched Shanna walk away, he drooled like a newborn baby. Shanna walked down a long, cold hallway toward the exit. Inmates stared and whispered as she brought them to fireballs of lust. Shanna acted like she didn't notice their lustful stares. This was her way of getting through the day without snapping. After making it to the exit, she realized she had left her car keys in her office.

Damn! Now I have to pass all these horny-ass niggas again," she thought before turning around and walking the plank again.

Shanna arrived at her office, grabbed her keys, and was on her way back out, when one of her students appeared at the door. Peter Saxon was an inmate who she spoke to a lot. He was truly gangsta; 'a boss' as some called him on the street. He was well known in the prison and feared by many guards and inmates alike. Peter, or P for short, was not an aggressive inmate on the surface, but he could have anyone touched from the jail to the streets with one word. This type of power frightened the warden and all of her counterparts.

P stood five feet, ten inches tall and was easy on the eyes. He was blessed with the silkiest black hair that could be imagined, and his waves spun like a raging sea. If one looked at his hair too long, they easily got seasick. He was always crisp; even in prison browns he had to be sharp. He recognized his power and walked in it on a regular basis.

The talk of the jail was his latest act of defiance, adorning his feet with the latest model of Louis Vuitton running shoes. This was what he called 'Boss Shit'. That act of defiance made top story on prison news due to the heaviness of the move. P liked when others recognized his G or respected his hand, as he often said. P wearing Louis Vuitton in the prison was heavy on so many levels. He had to have a guard or someone on payroll, and that was not a cheap thing to do.

P entered the office, took a seat, and began to hold a general conversation. Knowing where the conversation was headed, Shanna tried to hurry him along. He had been trying to get at her for a long time, but she was not indulging him. Not because she was not feeling him, but because she knew where their relationship would take her in the long run. Despite his failed advances, her and P remained cool.

"Where are you about to go, Ms. Butler?"

"I don't think I have to report to you," Shanna responded with a straight-up look. "Last time I checked, Mr. P, I didn't have a wedding ring on."

"No, you don't," he replied. "But, you know that engagement ring is only temporary. I'm just letting him borrow you until I get out."

They both laughed.

"Real shit, though, I just wanted to see how you were doing."

"I'm doing fine, but I'm sure that's not why you're here." She looked up and right into his eyes. "I know KM told you that I was here after he left my class."

KM, or Kevin Miller, was an inmate in her class. She took extra time to help him with his project, which he had to complete before he got paroled.

"Now that we got the bullshit out of the way," P said. "When you gonna be mine and let me hit that big ass? You know I get what I want."

Shanna frowned. "I think it's time for you to go now."

"We're both grown," P replied. "Why you looking like you don't know you got a big ass?"

"Goodbye, Peter."

P stood up and left out of the office. Shanna may have sent him away, but his presence lingered long after his exit. She walked away tingling all over.

Chapter 3

"Yo, what's up? I just left from seeing little homey."

"What's up wit 'em?" KM replied.

"Nothing much. We was just talking shit," P said. "Yo, come in and shut my door. You the fuck trippin'."

P and KM sat there shooting the breeze, blowing on some brown, and watching videos on his MP3 player. P held up his jailhouse cigarette and took two puffs. In between blowing out the smoke, he passed it to KM. They discussed crew shit and their plan to get at the people from the other crew for trying to infiltrate on their territory.

"KM, these niggas in here got the game messed up! This dude on D-unit has word out that he's about to take over the whole jail by any means necessary."

While sitting and listening like the pupil he was, "Word" was all KM managed to say in between drags.

P continued. "This guy has gotten a taste of the good life and is now being greedy. Word is that he's banging the little petite C.O. with the long, black hair on his unit, and now he thinks he's king of the world. Shit, I done banged almost every bitch in here, which means he has a lot of catching up to do."

"What C.O. are you talking about? Samuels?" KM questioned, then took the last drag of his cigarette.

"I think that's her name. She's a little too small for me. You know I like them big ol' ghetto booties! He can have those scraps."

Both men fell into laughter.

In prison, inmates acted as if they were on the streets. Men were judged on their money and the caliber of women that they pulled. Neighborhoods, jail-blocks, thoroughbreds, and weirdoes made up the different groups within the prison. The same caliber of niggas fraternized together. On rare occasions, a lame or weirdo snuck in the backdoor unknowing, but P's crew was tight...or so he thought.

"The jail is now in restricted movement!" a voice shouted through the loud speakers of the prison.

P was jarred back to the reality of him still behind bars. Looking out of his cell, he saw his fellow inmates being led like cattle to their respective cells. The block was painted pale beige with the officers' post in the center of the room. There were fifty cells that housed two inmates per cell, filling the block with one hundred men who were someone's son, nephew, cousin, and uncle. P was grief-stricken when he saw all of the black men that were "in the way" behind bars. None of his luxuries could cure the harsh reality staring him in the face. It was as if he'd seen his black brethren that way for the first time.

Following procedure, P fell back until the count was clear throughout the entire jail. He made use of his time while waiting to be let out of his cell by bagging up several pounds of weed. The weed was so pungent that he caught a contact from the smell alone. P kept black pepper sprinkled around his cell to hide the odor of the weed. The men on his crew, who were trained well, followed suite and stayed below the radar because of it.

P's numbers behind bars were unmatched. He had a connect who kept him laced with good product that had all the niggas in the jail spending their book and pick-up money on that shit.

P was in the groove as he bounced to the classic "All Eyez on Me" by 2PAC. He nodded his head while rocking back and forth. He was so into his task that he didn't notice his cell door being opened from the outside. When he placed the last bag in his stash spot, he turned around to meet the guard standing in his cell.

"Oh shit!" he proclaimed with his hand on his head. "You scared the shit out of me."

The guard responded with a stern order. "Get your ass up against the wall."

Following orders, P turned around, and the guard began to rub him in a seductive sexual manner. In response, P turned back around, pulled the guard close to him, and began to kiss deeply and passionately. His cellie knew the routine. He rolled over and placed his earphones on. P was in full glory and ready to stroke C.O. Paine until her shift was over.

Peggy Paine was a twenty-year veteran that had been on P's payroll and fuck list for a few years. Standing 5'4" and 140 pounds of shapely beauty, C.O. Paine was a fair-skinned, sexy, older woman that many of the inmates lusted over on a regular basis. Her full, puckered lips gave the appearance as if she was pouting. Her blonde and dark brown hair fell down to the middle of her back and changed from curly to straight depending on her mood.

"I been waiting for this nice stick all day. We have to hurry because my partner won't be in the bathroom long." Without another word, C.O. Paine dropped to her knees and took P's manhood in her mouth. She twirled and flicked her tongue on the tip of his rod until it jumped back on its own. P moaned and winced like a female getting pounded.

P loved her "twirlies", but he was one that needed to feel the warmth and tightness of some good sugar walls in order to be satisfied. So, he guided her head away from his crotch, picked her up, placed her on his lap, and then sat on the steel sink anchored on his wall. She rode him until his tip was bright red. P shook like an earthquake with a reading of ten on the Richter scale. His moans and her screams almost brought down the walls.

When C.O. Paine felt his rod swelling and about to release, she slid off of his lap, and the suction from her

26

tight cave echoed off the walls. She then slammed down on his manhood once more, backside first. P shook, and they both sung like two sopranos in a church choir. No more words were exchanged; they both had said enough.

C.O. Paine slipped out of his cell, while P lay in his bed enjoying the smell of sex in the air.

Chapter 4

Shanna continued to lunch with P on her mind. She was impressed by his drive and ambition, even if it was being used for so-called evil ways. P reminded her that lust still existed. She knew he was wrong for her. She was engaged, but her body ached like a tooth cavity whenever she was around him. Shanna still had a thing for bad boys, although she had sworn to give them up when she was faced with a terrible situation in her last bad-boy relationship.

Shanna had been involved with Corey Jenkins, one of the hardest thugs in her hood, for several years in high school. He came from a broken home, and his mother spent much of her time in the streets. Corey and Shanna went to the same teen club in their neighborhood. Shanna was a cool girl that had a lot of friends in and out of school. She got good grades, but still possessed a hood mentality. Corey did not attend her school because he was always locked up in juvenile detention centers, and when he was home, he went to an alternative school.

He and Shanna dated up until her senior year. That's when all hell broke loose. She had held out for a long time on saving her virginity, and with him being gone so much, it made it kind of easy. The majority of the summer before senior year, Corey stayed trouble free. They talked about moving away and him working while she went to college.

One hot summer night in his grandmother's basement, Shanna gave into her desire, and they made passionate love like they were full-grown adults. A day turned into weeks and then months, with Corey managing to keep out of trouble. Shanna's senior year had started, and Corey was set to go take his GED. The two could not get enough of each other physically and emotionally. They fucked like rabbits and had phone sex when they could not sneak away. For about a week, Corey had been keeping late hours and acting distant toward Shanna. She could not figure out what was going on.

It was a Friday night, and they had a scheduled date. Shanna decided she would confront Corey about his recent behavior. They went to a movie and fooled around in the park on the way home.

While laying in his arms and looking up at the fall sky, Shanna said, "Corey, what's up with your new attitude these past few days? I hope ya ass isn't out there slinging again."

It was at that moment that their happy evening turned sour quickly. Corey became very defensive, which proved he was up to something.

He pushed Shanna off of him and snarled, "You and your perfect fucking world! If I'm slinging again, it's my business. Everyone can't have a perfect life like you! Mine is fucked up, if you haven't noticed. A crackhead mother and a seventy-year-old grandmother on SSI is all I got. I can barely eat sometimes. Let alone keep my gear up! This life is not for me."

Shanna sat up straight as tears rolled down her face. She could not believe he was speaking to her that way, and more importantly, that he was barely living.

"I'm sorry, Cor. I didn't know. But, slinging is not the answer."

He wanted to reach out and dry her tears, but there was no one to dry his. He had to remain tough.

"Listen, don't feel sorry for me. You have a perfect world, and I don't. I have to take someone else's world and make it mine!" Corey said and then stormed off, leaving Shanna in the park alone crying hysterically.

The next morning, Shanna awoke for school, and as usual, she turned on her television to listen to the weather. As she was laying out her clothes for the day, the news switched from broadcasting the weather to a crime scene that showed body bags and bullet casings that were circled with chalk on the ground.

"Breaking news! A robbery gone bad has two people dead and two in critical condition in South Philly. Corey Jenkins, also known as Co-Jac, allegedly attempted to rob a known drug house. In the process, two people were killed, one being a Philadelphia police officer. Corey and his alleged accomplice are both in the University of Pennsylvania Hospital in critical condition. If they survive, they face murder one charges on two accounts. Sources revealed that Corey had just celebrated his eighteenth birthday and was attempting to straighten his life up. More on this story at noon."

A commercial came on after the news caster's report, and Shanna cried for what seemed like an eternity.

*****

Shanna did not pay attention to where she walked. Having always multi–tasked, she juggled at least three things at a time. While thinking naughty thoughts, she read her mail and contemplated what she would eat for lunch. She passed several co-workers, saying hello without looking up. After going through the last door, Shanna was brought to reality when she hit what felt like a brick wall. She tripped and sent her belongings in the air. When Shanna looked up, she saw the face of a husky brown-skinned woman with long black and grey hair. Shanna's papers flew out of her hands, and she apologized as she retrieved them from the floor.

"I'm extremely sorry. I was doing too much at once and did not see you."

Josie Evans stood watching Shanna pick up her belongings. Her face never changed throughout the exchange of words.

"My, my, you are in a hurry!"

"Yeah, I'm on my way to lunch."

Josie extended her hand. "Warden Evans."

"I'm sorry we had to meet like this," Shanna said as she shook her hand. "Ms. Shanna Butler," she told the warden, while pulling her hand back from the shake. "I'm a teacher and the head of Inmate Services here at the prison. Nice to meet you, Warden Evans. I came to your office to say hello a couple of weeks ago, but you weren't there."

Josie stood there and gathered herself. Then she cracked a half smile. "I'm pleased to meet you, but next time, watch where you're going. We don't need any workman's comp claims."

Shanna returned the half smile and produced a fake laugh. "See you later, Warden."

Shanna hurried to her car. She could not believe the new warden was so cold. She got in her 2007 Range Rover and pulled off so fast that the tires screeched.

The traffic was clear on the Roosevelt Boulevard Expressway. She was relieved because she only had an hour to meet her lunch date at Giannos' Italian Bistro. Thankfully, she made it downtown in ten minutes flat.

When Shanna jumped out of her truck, she almost broke a heel. She made it inside, but saw no sign of Tristen. Contemporary art decorated the walls in the bar area, and old-world Italian art hung on the walls in the dining area. Black and red satin tablecloths draped the tables. After taking a seat at the bar, a short blonde woman who was wearing all black approached her.

"Hello, Ms. Butler?"

"Yes."

"I'm sorry, but Mr. Stevens called and said he could not get out of an important meeting. He left his credit card number and said you could order whatever you want."

"Thank you."

Shanna was disappointed, just like she felt when she sat in her window waiting for her father who never showed up. Instead of staying to eat alone, she left the restaurant.

As she walked out the door, she bumped into a woman who was attempting to enter the restaurant.

"Sha?"

Shanna turned around with a big smile, knowing that only one person called her Sha.

"Trina? Oh my goodness! How long has it been?"

The ladies hugged.

Trina James had been a close childhood friend of Shanna's who she had lost touch with due to their different life choices. Trina was a high-yellow beauty with red freckles. She was all the guys' heartthrob from elementary school to college. By their second semester in college, Trina had fucked her way to getting straight A's. She had always been wild and loved the attention of the opposite sex.

Shanna was happy to see her friend, knowing that fun was Trina's middle name. Trina was just the person she needed to be around in order to get her mind off of Tristen's workaholic ass.

"Trina, you look good. What are you doing down here?"

Trina spun around, her Chanel halter dress spinning with her. She definitely was still an object of desire. Her long red hair flowed over her right shoulder in a deep wavy style.

"Thank you, and to answer your question, I'm down here for lunch. Why don't you join me?"

Shanna knew Trina would cheer her up with her wild stories about her traveling jaunts or one of her celebrity boyfriends.

"Okay, I guess I can chill a little while."

Trina and Shanna caught up on old times. Shanna let her know about her prominent boyfriend, but she refrained from being too open about her work at the prison. She knew Trina would be dramatic about

Shanna not pursuing her law degree after under-grad. That would stir up too many memories for Shanna, who was already feeling unfulfilled.

"Shit, you need to hook me up with one of those Mandingo niggas," Trina joked. "I need that in my life."

"Girl, you haven't changed a bit. Now what would you do with one of them not-having-a-job niggas? You too high maintenance for that!"

"Yes, I've changed a lot. My niggas now have more than seven zeros at the end of their bank account, and I get paid up front!"

As they both laughed out loud, Shanna looked down at her watch and realized she had been gone for almost two hours.

"Oh shit! Trina, I have to go if I want to keep my job. I'll holla at you later. You have my number. Call me."

Shanna left the table and walked to the valet. When she turned to give Trina a last goodbye wave, she got no response because Trina was engulfed in a conversation with a clean-cut white man who was dressed in an all-black Hugo Boss blended silk suit. Laughing to herself, Shanna continued on her journey.

Chapter 5

"Tristen Stevens for mayor! May I help you?"

Shanna hated when his secretary answered because that meant Tristen would not be available when she needed him.

"Yes, may I speak to Mr. Stevens?"

"Sorry, he is not available, Ms. Butler."

Shanna stared at her 3-karat princess-cut diamond set in platinum. She thought a lot about who Tristen was and wondered if she could deal with him always working and having limited time for her. Sure, she had given up the bad boys, but she now questioned if it was worth all the lonely nights.

Tristen, a 38-year-old mayoral candidate, stood over six feet tall. His skin was the color of milk chocolate, and his frame was solid. His eyes were captivating. They were the kind of eyes that swept women away and had them planning their honeymoon night in their daydreams. It was almost unbelievable that he was single, young, black, and powerful - even before he actually made it. He had made it through the primary elections and was now on his campaign trail for next fall, trying to take the position from the current mayor of the city.

Tristen had not been born with a silver spoon in his mouth. He was just hard working, smart, and in the right place at the right time. He got his start to greatness by blood, sweat, and tears alone. He grew up in Germantown on the east side of Philadelphia. His parents were both hard workers and stayed married until he was about thirty years old. His dad died from heart disease that was not detected until it was too late. As a result of his father being a janitor at a Villanova University, an Ivy League school in the suburbs of Philadelphia, Tristen was afforded the luxury of attending college for free. He graduated at the top of his class because his father pushed him to be the best he could be. Tristen continued his education and graduated with a Master's Degree in political science from the university. His father always told him that he was going to be in public office one day because of his fondness for world views.

Tristen became serious about running for office after his father's death. He felt he owed it to him, and Tristen vowed to make it happen.

His mother plugged him in with some prominent political figures. She was well connected in the political arena due to her being a strong community activist and the nanny to the senator's children. Tristen was now in the mayoral race in Philadelphia and prepared for the fight of his life.

Shanna was not at all concerned. She was confident that Tristen would make a wonderful mayor, whereas Henson, the current mayor and Tristen's competition, robbed the poor and fed himself and his people off of politics. Henson no longer needed to be mayor, and Shanna couldn't wait for her man to defeat him. Henson had been mayor for one term and was working hard to be re-elected. With her being on Tristen Stevens' arm, Shanna had her eye on the key to the city.

*****

Shanna returned to work and began sorting out things on her desk. She attempted to check her mail, when she heard a light tap. Shanna looked up.

"Come in," she said.

P entered the office, with his waves peaking through the sides of his kufi.

"Good morning, beautiful."

"How are you, P?"

"I'm hot and ready for some sweet Shanna"

Shanna felt herself grow warm at his presence. Tristen was missing in action, and she needed to be stroked.

"Look, if you're going to continue to disrespect me, you raise your ass up out of my office," Shanna said more so to convince herself than to scare P.

"Who you think you fooling? That ass is soaked. I know it is, and you know it is. But, I will let you get back to your work."

P exited her office, leaving Shanna's black lace thongs full of hot steam like a humidifier moistens the air. She was upset about her missing lover, but the day had to go on.

Shanna conducted a few specialty classes, completed the monthly service line up and the GED preparedness class. As she locked her classroom, she caught a glimpse of C.O. Branding, who she avoided like the plague. He was always trying to get in her panties and was one of the most negative people she had seen in a long time.

"Hello, sexy lady."

"Hi, Officer Branding."

"You know, I don't know why you even teach these nothing-ass niggas anything. They're in jail. What they need to be smart for? Now, if you need a student, I'm available after four o'clock."

Shanna felt her blood pressure rising at his stupidity and half-ass macking.

"I don't work after hours! Now, if you'll excuse me."

Shanna's workday was over, and she could not wait to make it to her destination. She had long forgotten about C.O. Branding's one-tooth ass comments. P's comments lingered far longer. They haunted her like the Ghost of Christmas Past. She damn near ran to her truck. She climbed in her platinum Range Rover, with her black Juicy skirt hugging all of her curves and her nipples poking against her silk Chanel shirt.

I got to get some dick soon, or I'm going to go crazy, she thought.

Shanna had an idea. After driving for a half an hour, she looked at her reflection in the rearview mirror and reapplied her favorite MAC lip gloss. Once she exited her vehicle, she looked up at the plush mirrored building and entered the lobby. While heading straight for the elevator, she started second-guessing her efforts.

"Fuck it. I'm going in," she said aloud.

Shanna entered the penthouse office and walked straight toward Tristen's office. She passed his secretary and swung the solid gold double doors open. Tristen, who was on the phone, looked up and smiled. Shanna locked the door behind her and took a seat in the big comfortable tan leather chair facing his desk. Tristen gestured that he would be off the phone in a second.

When he finally hung up the phone, he looked at Shanna with his smile displaying his pearly white teeth.

"What are you doing here?" he asked.

Shanna said nothing. She parted her legs to expose her bare, neatly trimmed wet box. His mouth opened like a cash register's drawer, and his eyes followed the line of her black fishnet thigh-high stockings.

"What…"

He was silenced by one of Shanna's soft, perky breasts. His manhood swelled and bounced like a ball as it pulsated. She slowly undressed him without speaking any words; her body did all of the talking. His bold, blue tie went first, which she used to blindfold her lover while he sat naked and ready for whatever.

Shanna bent over and mounted his lap backward. "Ooooooh," she said as her heated walls invited him in, welcoming his long, hard extension. She went up and down slowly, wanting to savor the moment. Tristen moaned as she circled her hips like she was hula-hooping.

Enjoying himself, Tristen didn't want the party to end so soon. So, he picked her up, laid her on his desk, and used his quick tongue for more than debating. He licked her pocket up and down, sucking her clit in between slurping. Shanna screamed and shook as he ushered climax after climax from out of her soul.

Chapter 6

"It's Friday, the money makin' day."

P had a problem locating his product.

"I know Beast did that shit. Always wanna fuck with me."

Beast, P's nemesis, had a guard on his payroll and on his lap, as well. In other words, he and P were on the same level. In prison, territory was still a big part of life. However, respect is larger than life; and neither man respected the other.

"That nigga fits his name in size only, black muthafucka."

Beast stood six feet tall with a muscular build. But, the nigga had no heart. He just liked to look like he did, and P knew it.

P motioned for KM to come to his cell.

"Listen, KM. I think that black-ass nigga stole my shit. I know nobody else got the balls to do something like that. He's mad 'cause I tagged his bitch a few times and almost snagged her to be the mule on my team. I need him to get the business, and I mean fuck him up good!"

KM had his assignment, and he wanted to prove his love for his squad. P had saved KM when he came straight from the juvenile detention center to the prison when he turned eighteen years old. He took him under his wing and protected him from getting his ass dug out, so KM was loyal to P.

KM was no fool. He was used to getting money on the street, and although he was loyal, he also knew offing Beast meant protecting his cash flow.

P strolled down the hall nodding his head to the few inmates he had conversation for. His swagger was wicked. Bitches loved him, and dudes wanted to be him. Everything about him, his walk, talk, and especially his python, had married women on a string.

P entered the yard and quickly scanned the inmates in the area. He was trying to place Beast and KM. Neither was in sight and that made P a little nervous. This was a big assignment and was supposed to send a message to all the other niggas with big ideas. P hoped KM was worthy of the job.

P sat on the bleachers with the rest of his crew, waiting on word from KM. While waiting, P relaxed and watched the basketball game. Two minutes later, KM came running across the yard with blood gushing from every opening of his face. Finally, KM reached a stunned P.

"I tried to execute the plan, but Beast and his peoples were waitin' for me." KM was gurgling blood while trying to explain what happened.

Blood poured from KM's face and splashed onto the bleachers. P leapt to his feet, partially because he was too vain to have someone's fresh blood on him and partially because he was ready to fuck Beast up.

A crowd started gathering in the far left corner of the yard, roaring as laughter filled the air. As P approached the crowd, he noticed one of Beast's bitches lying on the ground with his arm protecting his face. Beast stood over him acting like he was beating him, and the yard became hysterical with laughter.

Infuriated, P charged through the crowd swinging and punched Beast in the middle of his face. Before anyone realized what had happened, Beast lay on the ground as P's size twelve Timberlands redefined ass whoopin'.

A riot ensued, and guards yelled for the inmates to get down on the ground. Three seconds later, shots rang out and C.E.R.T., the Corrections Emergency & Riot Team, came in with force. Above their heads more shots rang out, warning the inmates to get down or be laid down.

P fell to the ground angry because he would mess up his fresh white tee and True Religion jeans that were hidden underneath his prison uniform pants.

When P glanced over at Beast and noticed his blank stare and that he wasn't breathing, he almost shit on himself. Murder was not his twist.

C.E.R.T. was all over the yard with rifles in their hands and stern looks on their faces. Inmates were being led back into the prison group by group. When the guards reached Beast, P's heart hit the ground.

"Beast, get the hell up!" the guard yelled.

"I can't feel my legs! My legs! Where are they?"

P breathed a small sigh of relief upon hearing Beast respond to the guard.

"Next time you'll keep ya muddy hands to yourself, Mr. Sticky Fingers. Fuck with my nigga again, and it'll be more than your legs you can't feel." C.O. Paine spit on Beast's forehead before motioning for the other guards to pick Beast up and take him away.

"P, get up and go back to your cell," Paine instructed, her voice dripping with seduction.

After all the inmates were in their cells, the call for restricted movement came over the loud speaker. It was strange to hear the warden's voice give the order.

While removing his now dirty shirt, a soft vibration went off in P's pants. P forgot he had his cell phone on his hip. He looked at the caller ID before answering.

"Yeah."

"Nigga, don't *yeah* me. What the fuck is the problem, and why can't you handle ya business better than that?" a high-pitched voice shouted at him.

P wanted to reach through the phone and smack the shit out of the bitch.

"Bitch, calm down. I have control of my shit."

"Oh yeah? I can't tell. KM has a broken nose, a three-inch cut above his left eye, and three cracked ribs.

And Beast? That nigga will be lucky to walk in the next week or two. So, please, please, tell me how you have your shit under wraps."

P massaged his temples and breathed in deeply. He tried to remember the techniques Ms. Butler taught in her class about coping skills that helped in stressful moments such as this.

Once again, P attempted to calm the caller down, " I can and will handle my end. Just handle your end and stop harassing me. Now, let me get back to my shit!"

He flipped closed his phone and started pacing around his cell.

What went down at the drop and why? How did Beast know? I'ma get that muthafucka, I swear, P thought as he put in his earphones.

*****

The phone rang. Lieutenant Greenwich answered it, got his orders, and marched straight to the infirmary.

He entered the infirmary with disgust building in his throat and his teeth grinding. Greenwich was tired of being the sweeper. However, the call came from his superior, and he valued his job.

Greenwich spotted Beast being tended to by a nurse who had breasts bigger than Dolly Parton's. With a big huff, the lieutenant strolled up to Beast and crossed his arms as he gestured for the nurse to leave them alone. Once she was gone he leaned closer to Beast.

"So what happened and who did it?"

"Do I look like I know what happened? I can barely see out of my eyes. However, I know you will do your best to apprehend all those who were involved," Beast said in the most proper voice he could manage.

Lieutenant Greenwich's face turned cherry red.

"So you think you're being cute?

Greenwich stepped closer to Beast, aligning his nose tip-to-tip with Beast's nose. He really wanted to smack the shit out of the fool, but he knew he had to refrain.

"Whatever ya issue is, it needs to be addressed and then you need to move on. Make sure that money is available when scheduled. This is comin' from the boss. I hate your kind and detest being involved in this shit, so don't push me!" Greenwich patted Beast on the right shoulder and left.

Beast lay back on the hospital bed with pain shooting from his legs to the crown of his head.

That nigga gave me good workout, but I'll return the favor in due time, he thought.

Beast was a little confused about exactly what bullshit KM was talking. Beast didn't know anything about P's drop being intercepted. KM even had the nerve to attempt to steal his shit. After trying several times to explain this to KM, Beast had a few of his bitches take care of him.

Beast was drowsy from the painkillers and beat down from the waltz with P. He gave in to the struggle with the inevitable as his eyes closed.

Lieutenant Greenwich left the infirmary and walked to his office. He knew the warden would be on his phone in a matter of minutes. Before opening the door to his office, Ms. Butler waved her hand in the air hoping to get his attention.

"Yes, Ms. Butler?" The lieutenant dragged her name out to show how irritated he was with her.

Shanna stopped and momentarily stared at the lieutenant with a confused look. In an attempt to remain calm, she tapped her cream-colored Kenneth Cole ankle boots on the floor and brushed the palm of her hands against her powder pink BCBG trousers.

"Hello, Lieutenant Greenwich. I was just wondering why the jail was shut down."

"Obviously, the inmates weren't good boys today."

Through tight lips, Shanna responded, "Yes, that may be obvious, but what's not so obvious is what the inmates did wrong."

"There was a fight between P and Beast. Some blood was shed, ribs cracked, and noses broken. But, don't worry. P is okay."

"Thanks," she simply responded.

Shanna knew the lieutenant was coming at her neck, but she refused to entertain him. So, she turned and switched her bubble ass back down the hall. Once at her office door, Shanna put her key into the lock, but not before peeking back at Lieutenant Greenwich. She giggled to herself because she had caught him staring at her beautiful backside. Feeling like a fool, Greenwich entered his office just as his phone was ringing.

"Lieutenant Greenwich. Can I help you?" he snorted into the phone.

"You don't sound happy. Why is that? Wait! Let me answer that one for you. The jail is locked down, and my two key moneymakers are fucked up. Now, I know why I'm not happy, but why aren't you happy?" The voice was calm but irritated.

The sound of a No. 2 pencil tapped against the weathered down wooden desk that furnished the lieutenant's office. He was nervous, yet he knew he had to give an answer and quick.

"Well, I think that—" The lieutenant didn't have a chance to finish his statement before being cut off.

"Listen, my money better be right, and get it to me on time or I'm comin' for your balls."

Click!

The lieutenant leaned back in his swivel chair and closed his eyes. He imagined stuffing tube socks into the warden's mouth and then duct taping her to a rusty pole. He knew he should have been up on things, but damn…she don't do shit and was always complaining. He quickly wondered how she would fair if a leak to the paper explained how there was a riot at the prison with no punishment for the perpetrators. How would she look then?

STAR

The warden was knee-deep in horseshit, yet she still smelled like roses. Things were going to have to change.

Chapter 7

"FOOLS! I work with pure fools!"

The warden paced the floor and then threw herself in the red, oversized loveseat, landing on her back. She was trying to decide on what medicine to take for the huge headache the incompetent assholes had given her. She tried to kick her shoes off onto the floor, but she was only half successful in the attempt. One shoe flew back, heading for her face, but she managed to block it, causing it to land on the coffee table.

"I'm so happy I didn't choose the tinted green glass top," the warden whispered to herself.

Her phone rang, and Josie skated across the room full of anticipation. After flopping down in her leather computer chair, Josie took two deep breaths and lifted the receiver.

"This is Warden Evans. How can I be of assistance?"

"Josie, why do you act like you don't know it's me calling? I call you at the same time every day. Anyway, how is my pussycat doing?" a deep, mature voice inquired.

Josie looked down at her one-karat Liz Claiborne watch and nodded her head in agreement to the caller. She always had a hard time answering her lover. Butterflies fluttered in her stomach and giggles took residence in her throat. She stole a deep glance at the many portraits that decorated her marble top desk. She couldn't help but feel sad. It nerved her that she couldn't place a picture of herself and her lover on her desk. Shit, she couldn't convince him to take a snapshot to furnish her mantelpiece at home.

"I know it's you, but I'm at work. To answer your question, I'm fine now that your voice has graced my longing ear."

"HA! HA! HA! You got to be kidding!" He laughed so hard he started to choke.

Josie's shoulders slumped over, allowing her hair to rest on her right cheek. She couldn't understand how insensitive her man could be at times.

"Josie, baby, I'm sorry. Please forgive me."

"It's fine," she muttered.

"Good. Let's get down to business. How's that project coming along?"

"It's coming along."

"Josie, don't be coy with me. How far along are you, and when will I be hearing something in the media? Election day seems far away, but it will be here before you know it."

He's such an asshole at times. Insults and demands in the same breath just don't go together.

"I shouldn't do shit, but I'm working on the deal and everything is coming along. It shouldn't more than a week or so."

"Yeah, well, this boy is on my neck, and unless something happens fast, I'll be out of a job. Pop some pills. Snort some coke. Do whatever it takes to get some speed in your step."

Obviously, her lover's tone wasn't going to get any sweeter unless she said what he wanted to hear.

"Sweetheart, I have everything under control. She will go down and take your competitor with her."

"That's what I needed to hear, Josie, but you never did answer my question."

"What question was that?" Josie asked, a little confused.

Henson chuckled and said, "How's my pussycat doing?"

It was amazing how Henson could still make her feel like a schoolgirl. Josie's cheeks were red as ripe tomatoes, and her breathing became shallow. Josie walked across the cramped office and stood anxiously in front of her leather couch. She knew it was inappropriate, but she desperately desired to relax on the couch and play with her womanhood.

Henson knew any mention of sex would snatch Josie's tongue. He'd rather initiate phone sex instead of having to pop Viagra to mount Josie. It was like fucking a man. Josie always wanted him to toss the salad and then put Big Johnson in the dungeon. To top it off, Josie's body was hard as a cement wall. Still, it was cute how he could make Josie be at a loss for words.

"Are you still there?" Henson whispered.

Josie felt an instant gush, and her boy shorts were wet as if she had urinated on herself. Josie jumped onto the couch, throwing one leg over the arm of the couch and allowing her left leg to dangle. She positioned herself to do just as Henson suggested.

"Henson…baby, talk to me. I need to hear your voice."

Henson had to control himself from laughing. He felt like Jamie Foxx was doing a stand-up comedy show just for him.

After clearing his throat, Henson told her, "Imagine a peppermint rolling around in my mouth as I slowly approach you from behind. You're entertaining me by rotating your ass in the air. Before I place my face between your full thighs, I notice your long, delicate fingers have beat me to the job."

Henson began to breathe in deep and slow. He was now imagining Josie bouncing up and down on Big Johnson with enough force to excite a senior citizen home.

Using two fingers, Josie rubbed her cave with even strokes. She loved when Henson used a mint; the combination of his cool breath and the peppermint sent a warm sensation throughout Josie's body. Her nipples would get so hard that they ached, and Josie would have to swallow two 600 milligrams of Motrin after one of their sessions.

Josie couldn't control her panting. She really wanted Henson to rock her world. It was hard for Josie to resist the urge to toot her ass in the air.

"Baby, please don't stop. I'm almost there."

So was Henson. Big Johnson demanded to be released, and Henson obliged by dropping his Ralph Lauren slacks and boxers to the newly polished wooden floor of his office. Henson didn't need any Vaseline; he used the juices he had already released. This shit was getting so good that Henson had to use both hands to handle his manhood. Surprisingly, Josie's breathing and demands made his rod swell more.

"Wooooo, turn that fat ass over so I can invade Alexandria. My stick is going to part your ass like Broad Street. First, I want you to juggle me in your mouth and slide your fingers down my cave."

71

Josie hesitated for a minute. Henson's ass had more fur than a full-grown bear. The thought of her fingers near his butt interrupted her flow.

Trying to keep her mind steady, Josie answered, "I want you to tickle my clit and then beat up my ass!"

Both Henson and Josie's air supply was cut off while they climaxed. Henson's hand pumped quicker than a lion racing to kill his prey. Josie's left hand provided the sensation to her lizard while she tried to pump her right hand in and out of her hole.

Josie wanted to fall asleep on her cream-colored hand-woven rug. That was not an option she had work to do.

"Baby, are we still on tonight for dinner?"

Josie held her breath while waiting for him to answer. He had cancelled their regular dinner the last four times, and she was starting to get concerned. The last time this happened, it was because his wife had threatened a divorce. Josie didn't see him for over two months during that time.

"Yes, love. Meet me at Moshulu at seven-thirty sharp. See you then."

Josie perked up. *What am I going to wear? How am I going to do my hair? What perfume should I choose?* She had so many things to do in such little time.

First, she had some things to line up, though. Before the week was out, Butler was going down and her fiancé with her! After reminding herself that she was doing it for love, Josie hesitated before reaching for her all-white Fendi bag to pull out her cell phone and dial a number.

"Yeah, give the package to number one and have him place it in the storage room adjacent to Ms. Butler's office. Make sure Lieutenant Greenwich gets wind of the situation."

After giving the order, Josie hung up and made sure to put the phone back in her handbag. Nervous, heartless, or mischievous? Josie couldn't quite put her finger on the feeling she had in her chest.

With it being the end of the workday, Josie rose from her chair, grabbed her purse and jacket, and exited her office. On her way out of the prison, she purposely walked past Ms. Butler's office and looked through the door's glass panel before entering.

"Ms. Butler, please make sure all reports you have on Peter Gardner are placed in his file. And don't forget the new folders are in the storage room. Be sure to transfer all of Mr. Gardner's information before leaving his file in my box tonight. I expect everything to be done before morning." Josie then turned and left, closing the door behind her.

Shanna took a few seconds to gather her thoughts before running down the dimly lit hall to catch the warden before she exited the building. As Shanna turned the left corner, she saw the warden and Lieutenant Greenwich whispering. The lieutenant seemed a little concerned, his eyes darting back and forth as he rubbed his hands roughly against his uniform pants. Lieutenant Greenwich spotted Shanna before she could disappear back around the corner.

"Yes, Ms. Butler?"

"I apologize for…"

"What? You apologize for trying to eavesdrop on a private conversation?" Warden Josie said.

"No, I was going to apologize for something else. However, I think you, Warden, should be handing out the apologies."

The lieutenant leaned against the counter and fixed his gaze downward to the cold marble floors. Josie shifted her weight from one foot to the other and repositioned her pocketbook.

"Goodnight, Lieutenant," Josie said, then walked out of the building without acknowledging Shanna's comment.

Shanna was livid. She stomped up the hall like a two-year-old having a tantrum. Once she reached her office, she slammed the door shut behind her and let out a low growl.

"That bitch must have been slipped a mickie. Who the fuck does she think she's dealing with? I'll bust that bitch's ass. Fuck her!"

As she pulled files from her cabinet, the phone's ringing infuriated her even more.

"YES, THIS IS BUTLER!"

"Sweetheart, why are you yelling?" Tristen asked.

"Oh, my apologies. Everything is fine. How are you, darling?"

"I'm pretty sure something is wrong, and I'm pretty sure if I ask what's wrong, you'll say nothing."

Shanna disagreed with Tristen. "Baby, I'm fine, but I have to go so I can finish all this work the warden from hell has given me to do. So, I'll talk to you soon."

Shanna worked at a steady pace to complete her task. She hated the warden and wanted to tell her to go screw herself, but she took her job seriously and did not want to seem insubordinate. Tristen knew Shanna well. With him being understanding and passionate about everything he was involved in, that's why Shanna loved him. She did not want to worry him about her petty power struggles with the new warden.

Finally done writing her reports, Shana packed her supplies away and headed out of her office to locate the files the warden mentioned. She entered the storage room in search of the new files. She located them then quickly returned to her office. The lieutenant and two other corrections officers entered the storage room after Shanna went into her office. Lieutenant Greenwich stood by and watched Shanna exit the storage room. He was sure to have the security camera in the corridor face the room. A short while later, the lieutenant recruited a couple of rookie officers to conduct a routine search. They quickly emerged from the storage room with an unidentified wrapped package.

*****

Across town, Josie was happy and preparing for her dinner date with Henson. She was putting on her dress, when her phone rang.

"Hello?"

"Don't worry, I'm still going to make it to dinner, but there will be someone else attending, also."

"Henson…"

"It'll be the governor. You know he's a supporter in my race against Tristen," Henson responded matter-of-factly.

"Okay, I will see you then, honey."

She hung the phone up in disgust. *Who does Henson think he is?* Josie couldn't help but wonder if she was the only one in this relationship.

Josie took her sweet ol' time getting dressed. She refused to put on perfume, knowing that would upset Henson.

After leaving her house, Josie sat behind the wheel of her vintage Rolls Royce, watching as the time changed on the clock. She then put the car in reverse and drove to her date.

Chapter 8

Like clockwork, the alarm went off at 6:00 a.m., waking Shanna out of a beautiful dream; diamonds falling from the sky while she skipped through a lily pasture. She laughed out loud at the remembrance.

Shanna didn't want to leave her 600-thread count Egyptian sheets. She sighed and rose from the bed. Shanna showered and dressed quickly so she could have some time to talk to Tristen before their day started. After spraying on her favorite perfume, she looked herself over in the mirror.

"Perfect," she said aloud.

She glanced at her watch and reached for her phone. The phone rang three times before Tristen picked up.

"This is Tristen."

"Good morning, baby. I didn't think I was going to talk to you."

"Well, you got me, and I'm glad you did. I forgot to remind you about the debate I'm having with Henson at the YMCA." Tristen was breathing hard like an overweight runner.

"Okay, I'll be there, but when are we going to meet up for some debating of our own?"

"Look, Shanna, my other line is beeping, so I'll talk to later. Better yet, I'll see you at the debate. Bye, babe. I love you." Tristen hung up before answering her question.

She stared at the phone and shook her head. *I know he loves me, but damn, he has a funny way of showing it,* she thought while gathering up her teaching materials. *Maybe I'll call Trina and see if she wants to bless Club Denim with me.*

After loading the car with all the things she needed for the day's lesson, Shanna jumped into the driver's seat and blasted Beyoncé's "Upgrade You" before pulling out of the driveway. In a good mood, she danced and sang all the way to the prison.

"Yeah, I'm going to have to hit Trina up by lunchtime. I'm ready to shake what my momma gave me."

The heels of Shanna's Luca Luca shoes created a beat against the concrete and the hard floors of the prison's waiting room. Before she could enter, though, she had to be searched. Sometimes, she felt the searches were a little extreme.

Officer Paine sat at the desk, seemingly in a good mood. Then she saw Shanna standing at the door. Paine looked through her.

"Paine, can you please buzz me in?" Shanna shifted her weight to her right leg and tilted her head.

Snapping her neck around to face Shanna, Paine responded, "I'm in the middle of something, so you will just have to wait."

After a few minutes, Paine hit the button. The women stared at each other before Paine searched her.

I ought to put a pencil through Paine's right temple, Shanna thought.

After the search had been conducted, Shanna smiled and said, "Thanks, Paine," then walked to her office.

As Shanna entered the block, she received whistles and comments from the inmates who were mingling about regarding what she had blessed with from her mama. She smirked but ignored the comments. Once Shanna made it to her office, she sat at her desk and turned on the computer.

Knock. Knock.

When she looked up, her eyes saw something so stunning that Shanna had to squeeze her legs together to control herself.

"What's up, Ms. Butler? How is your day starting?" P smiled, showing off his pearly whites.

Shanna wanted to body slam him on her desk and rip off his pants. Instead, she swallowed hard and waved for P to come in the office.

"Don't yell across the room. Come and sit down, Gardner."

P was all too happy to oblige.

"So when are you going to let me—"

"Listen, don't come in here with that. When are you going to add words to your vocabulary? I'm a little tired of the same questions."

P leaned back in the chair and crossed his legs. He had to think first before answering Shanna. P was a little surprised she came at his neck like that, but he could understand where she was coming from. Shanna just made him feel like he was a young bull.

"Alright, alright, I get the message, Ms. Butler."

P stood up to leave the office before Shanna made him feel smaller than he already felt.

"Where are you going? We need to talk about the show you put on the other day." Shanna looked P straight in the face and saw him flinch.

"It wasn't my show. It was Beast's show. I was just a cast member. I really don't want to talk about it.

"Okay, but we will have to handle this later."

When Shanna walked P to the door, she noticed that Paine was in the hall staring at the two of them. Paine's face was twisted in a knot. Shanna looked at Paine and then P. As she started putting two and two together, she shook her head.

Whatever, she thought.

P left Shanna's office ready to play with his piece. Her round, shapely ass made his dick pulsate. P was thinking so hard about Shanna that he walked by Paine without noticing her.

Paine sucked in her breath as P passed her without speaking. Then she turned her attention toward Shanna's office and stared. *Bitch is trying to get with my thang. Humph. We'll see about that,* she thought as she walked to her station.

P walked the hall until he reached the storage closet located in the laundry room that held all of the cleaning supplies. Only certain inmates were allowed on laundry patrol and cleaning duty, and since he was one of the elite, he had full access. He opened the door and walked to the rear of the closet to retrieve a broom so he could sweep his cell. When he heard voices approaching, he hid in the closet.

"Look, we have to do it exactly the way he said or he might have us taken care of."

"Nigga, stop being a bitch. We can take half of the stash and still handle our business. What's the problem?"

"No, we will follow the plan. Do you remember where P and that nigga KM is suppose to be at two?"

Even though the two voices were whispering, P could hear them loud and clear. The problem was he couldn't place faces with the voices and trying to get a look would expose him.

I know Beast is behind this shit, P thought. *Looks like a murder is about to go down.*

After the perpetrators left, P waited a few minutes before opening the closet door. He looked around and then walked down the hall, making eye contact with everyone who looked suspicious. Everybody in the jail was suspect. He was on high alert, refusing to trust anybody because anybody could be the one to stab him in the back, literally. P listened to every voice as he passed prison browns, uniforms, and plain clothes. It seemed like an eternity before P reached his cell. Carefully, P scanned his cell before entering.

"Yo, wassup?"

P turned around and snatched his shank from under his mattress. "Nigga, you almost got that shit that make your bowels loose."

Ignoring P, KM walked into the cell and sat on the lower bunk. "Like I said, what's up?"

"What's up is ya boy is trying to set us up. I overheard some niggas talking shit."

"What? P, for real?" KM said. Dread crept across his face and his neck muscles tensed.

"Fool, I know you ain't scared."

"Naw, I ain't scared. I got two bodies under my belt," KM responded as he pounded his right fist in his left hand.

"Alright, go get everybody rounded up and have them meet me at the spot."

KM nodded and walked out the cell. After stepping only a few feet, he ran into two inmates, one wielding a handmade knife and the other carrying a long piece of rope. KM had no time to react as P hit one dude in the head with a hardcover book and kicked the other in his right hip. He was confused at how these niggas was on his block unsecured like they belonged there. KM turned around confused, watching as P stomped the men.

Seeing four other guys running towards them, KM leaped over P and hit the first of Beast's messengers that crossed his path. Beast tapped on the window alerting the C. O. on duty it was time to earn his keep. The C.O. allowed him to gain access and walked away from the area. Beast entered P's block and rushed to the crowd, his eyes focused on P.

P's clique rushed toward the fight as P fucked up anybody in his way. "Y'all don't know who you're fuckin' with!" P shouted as he threw another punch.

P looked to the right and saw KM stomping one of Beast's men. He then looked left and saw Beast entering the area. That caught his attention. At the same time, KM, who saw Beast take a swing at his cellmate, decided he wanted Beast for himself. KM had revenge to get.

The mayhem in the block was intense. P and KM both tried to get to Beast, but neither man could reach him. P knew C.E.R.T. would be there soon, so he got as much work in as possible on everyone else.

Shanna heard the call for the jail to be locked down again.

These fools can never get through a day without bullshit, Shanna thought while shaking her head.

Shanna poked her head into the hallway. The hall was clear; there weren't any guards in sight. So, she went back to her desk and grabbed her phone, knowing she wouldn't see any inmates for a while.

When C.E.R.T. arrived, they came in with sticks, shields and teargas. P got slammed in the ribs and pushed back to his cell. KM saw C.E.R.T. and found his opportunity. He pulled his knife and kept low to the floor. Beast's back was to KM, but that didn't matter as KM dug into Beast's neck. KM stabbed Beast four times and one of his soldiers twice in the heart before he dropped the knife and retreated. The cameras on the unit had malfunctioned thanks to Beast's C.O. on duty. C.O. Samuels let out a loud scream and ran towards the fallen inmate. KM made it to his cell without C.E.R.T. snatching him up. Once there, he fell to his bed to relax.

The boss will be happy, KM thought.

*****

After Shanna hung up her phone, she went to the restroom. She'd had to pee for about an hour, but couldn't use the restroom because of the prison riot. Shanna was in the handicap stall when a C.O. entered. She was in tears and talking on her cell phone.

"Girl, this place is driving me crazy! The jail is locked down because these fools were fighting and someone was stabbed to death." Tears streamed down her face as she confided in her friend on the phone. "Girl, Greenwich got me sucking his dusty balls and bringing illegals in."

Shanna stayed quiet. *This shit is crazy,* she thought. When she realized the riot took place on P's cellblock, she wanted to go check on him

"I tried to tell the lieutenant I didn't want this shit anymore, but he's hanging over my head how he caught me in Beast's cell, half dressed and breathing heavy. Now he stabbed up and I don't know if he will survive and shit. If I get fired, who's going to take care of my kids? Their dads ain't shit."

Shanna's first thought was to open the stall door and offer some advice, but something held her back.

"No, I'll be alright. Let me go before I'm hunted down. I'll call you later." The C.O. hung up the phone and stared at herself in the mirror for a few moments. A tear-stained, confused face stared back. She washed her face, straightened her clothes, and left the bathroom.

Shanna waited in the stall long enough to make sure the C.O. had left. Then she washed her hands and returned to her office. As she unlocked her door, she heard the phone ring. Shanna ran across the office to her desk.

"This is Ms. Butler. How can I help you?"

"Girl, you sound out of breath. Stop swinging on those house dicks and save some for me."

Shanna laughed and sat in her chair.

"I got your message. I'm down whenever you are." Trina was always ready to party, and it had been a long time since her and Shanna hung out together.

"We can go tonight after Tristen's debate. His debate should be over by seven-thirty. That will give me some time to relax before meeting you at the club. This is an upscale place called Club Denim. Christie Denim, a prominent socialite from Europe, owns it. The men are fine and wealthy...for you, of course."

"Oh okay, for me?" Trina said, then emitted a short laugh. "Anyway, girl, Tristen is probably going to want to chill with you after the debate. We can do this another day."

"No, we'll go out tonight. Fuck what Tristen wants."

"Whatever is good for you, Shanna, but don't bring that 'I'm-depressed-over-my-man and need to talk' shit to the club. We can save that for a cup of coffee."

"Bye, Trina!"

Shanna gathered her belongings and walked out her door, She saw Lieutenant Greenwich talking with Samuels in the hall. Without glancing back, Shanna continued down the hall.

Shanna addressed them as she walked bye. "Good evening. I'll see everyone tomorrow."

She fought traffic to get to the YMCA. As she pulled into a parking space, she felt a migraine coming on. She rubbed her temples and searched for some pain medicine in her purse. She grabbed a bottle of water from back seat and threw two Motrin in her mouth. After swallowing the pills, she got out the car.

Once inside, Shanna searched for Tristen and saw him speaking with a group of supporters. She walked toward the group undetected. She noticed posters of Tristen hanging. The message scrawled on them, Tristen Stevens for Mayor Today - and In the White House Tomorrow, gave her a slight twinge. She knew if he actually did run for president one day, their time together would be limited even more.

Shanna walked up behind two women and said, "I have a question. What do you plan to do about parking at the YMCA?"

Tristen smiled and motioned for Shanna to come to him.

"Everyone, this is my future wife, Shanna Butler."

Shanna waved to the crowd. The women smirked.

"The speech is about to begin. Everyone, please file into the auditorium," Tristen said. Then he and Shanna walked over to a corner where they could have a moment together.

"Good luck, babe." Shanna kissed him on the cheek.

He smiled and said, "Thank you."

Then they parted; Shanna to her seat, and Tristen to the stage.

"Okay, Mr. Stevens, you won the coin toss. So, the questions will start with you. What do you plan to do about the excessive crime on the streets?"

Clearing his throat, Stevens answered, "This question has a two-part answer. First, I would fund more afterschool programs that will focus on keeping children off the streets. Secondly, I believe the community would benefit from having more police officers right on the street- the public's foot soldiers."

The room erupted with applause, with Shanna's being the loudest. As she looked around the crowd to check their expressions, her eyes landed on Warden Josie sitting in the corner of the room. They locked eyes, and the warden shifted. Her expression was that of a child who had gotten caught with their hand in the cookie jar. While continuing to clap, Shanna turned her attention back to Tristen.

Tristen was doing well, but it appeared as if his response didn't interest his competitor. The mayor, Henson Williams III, closed his eyes. In reality, Henson's insides were quivering because he knew this young bull was giving him a run for his money, and he hadn't packed his running shoes.

Even though Shanna was there to support Tristen, she watched the clock like a Christian does in the middle of a long sermon. She refused to miss her girls' night out. Why should she? Tristen didn't put anything to the side for her.

Chapter 9

"What the fuck! What's going on?" Trina shouted over the alarm that went off. It sounded as if there was a live concert in her bedroom. "Who the hell set the alarm?"

With her eyes still closed, Trina stretched an arm out and wiggled her fingers, hoping to reach the alarm without having to get out of the bed. Finally, her fingertips completed the search, and Trina beat every button until the blaring music was silenced.

Deciding it was time to start the day, Trina swung her smooth legs off the bed and sat on the side. She slid her feet back and forth across the cool floor to locate her crystal-studded slippers. In her failed attempt to locate them, Trina sucked her teeth and rolled back into bed, using the teal satin sheets to shelter her face from the sunlight that bullied itself through the curtains.

It took Trina a few more seconds before she realized the bed she was occupying wasn't her own. Sitting straight up, Trina darted her eyes around the room. The bedroom was simple; however, elegance shaped the room. Cream and brown marble decorated the floor with the assistance of an oval, multi-colored floral rug. The bed and fireplace sat in the center of the perfectly square room.

"Whoever this guy is, he must be a romantic," Trina thought aloud. She could just imagine making love while flickering lights from the fireplace performed on her nude body.

Trina redirected her gaze to the wall art. Pictures of a baby being held by strong, lean hands decorated the entire wall on the far left side of the room. However, what were breathtaking were the tall windows that allowed natural light to invade the room. Sheer lilac curtains carefully swept the floor whenever nature blew a gentle breeze.

Trina scooted across the bed and then walked over to the inviting windows. Allowing the curtains to wrap around her, she entered the showcase of the world below her. The streets were littered with people, vehicles, pets, and flashing traffic signals. Lovers walked hand-in-hand, while others fussed over the lack of parking spaces.

The view of the city helped Trina figure out what neighborhood she was in, and from there, she was able to guess what condo building's window she was peering out. Continuing to enjoy the scenery, Trina used her fingernails to comb through her hair as the locks of curls danced along her back and tickled her full breasts. Trina stood in the window with her favorite outfit on—her birthday suit. Her flawless body with its perfect measurements was the reason why she was able to rock nothing but the best designer clothing, drive the hottest cars, and reside in several parts of the world. In other words, Trina could afford whatever her heart desired.

Reality tapped Trina on the shoulder when she heard the voice of a gentleman call her from the next room. After one final look at the city, Trina followed the voice. She didn't have to go far, though, because her trick was standing in the doorway of the bedroom.

Trina had to admit the man was the epitome of sexy. Her "hot pocket" did flips while she stared at all six feet of the brown-skinned, wavy-haired, hazel-eyed, muscle-sculpted creature standing before her. Everything was clear now: Trina remembered meeting Mr. Glamorous at the Denim Club. Shanna and Trina had gone out together, but Shanna got all lovesick and left early. So, Trina left solo with a job.

Trina remembered drinking more than her share of drinks. Shit, why not, and especially since they were free. Shanna and Trina danced, drank, danced, and drank some more. It was obvious they were two girls who had come to party.

The gentleman who continuously eyed Trina sent drinks over all night, and by the end of the night, Trina wanted to express her gratitude. So, she met the man at the bar, and in her state of being inebriated, she kissed him like they were lovers.

Now him just standing in the doorway made her recall the entire evening.

"You are just how I love my women—naked!" he sang, then started to approach Trina.

This fool must be stupid. Don't he know how much my time cost? she thought.

"Is that right?" Trina replied, folding her arms across her bare breasts.

"Yeah, so I'm going to need you to relax on the bed for a rubdown."

Trina couldn't believe someone could lack that much imagination.

"First, you're going to have to pay for last night and now," she said.

"Well, I already paid for last night, and I thought I was good enough for one free shot."

"Baby, there is no one on this earth good enough for one *free* shot."

"Okay, well, how about one thousand?" he asked.

"What do you want me to do, rub your back? I don't get out of bed for anything less than three thousand."

"So, three grand it is."

Trina walked over to her handbag to check and see if prior payment had been made. Satisfied with the form of payment and the amount, Trina said, "Lay flat on your back. If you touch me with your hands one time, I'm getting up. Understand?"

"Yeah, yeah. Okay, enough talking."

Trina walked to the bed, and with her back facing him, she slowly lowered her wet-box directly over his face. As if obeying a command, he licked and sucked her moisture like a starving African. Trina could barely concentrate on her next move due to the oral pleasure she was receiving. Finally, she managed to tilt the top half of her body forward until her juicy lips met his hard, long drill. Trina covered his throbbing rocket with her mouth and massaged his balls with one hand. She licked, sucked, and toyed with him until his legs almost locked. Then Trina flipped around, mounted him, and slid down his piece like she was dancing on a million-dollar pole. Her hips took over, and in ten minutes, Trina made him launch a liter of cum. He quickly fell asleep afterwards.

As Trina crawled off of him, her cell phone rang.

"Yeah."

"Did I reach Trina?" a deep voice asked.

"Yeah."

"Well, I heard you were the best in the business. I have a project that will prove worthy of your time, Ms. Trina."

Trina looked back at sleeping beauty before walking down the long hallway where she found the bathroom. She entered the baby-blue restroom and sat on the side of the tub.

"Go on."

"There's a young man that I have on staff, and I have been working the hell out of him. As a gift, I would like to give him a night to remember."

"I can fulfill your employee's wildest dreams, but the wilder the night, the more my fee will be."

"Fine. Just make sure his dreams aren't fulfilled past twenty grand."

Trina choked after hearing the offer.

"That's not a problem. Someone will have to meet with me before the show takes place, though. Also, I want all hundred dollar bills." Trina took a few breaths before asking, "Is there anything in particular you would like for me to wear, do, say, or provide?"

He contemplated for a few moments. "Since you asked, I would like for you to wear a black strapless dress, a pair of lace crotchless panties, and no bra. Wear your hair in a long ponytail, something good to pull on. Oh yeah, beverage and food will be provided."

"Not a problem. Where and when would you like for this to happen?" Trina asked, anxious to perform the services so she could get paid.

"This evening, if it's not too soon."

"I'm on your time, not mine, love," she responded.

"Eight o'clock sharp at the Hilton. Please be on time. Someone will meet you at the front desk and take you to the room."

"Like I said, I'm on your time," Trina repeated before hanging up. *I wonder who the baller was that called,* she thought while skipping to the bedroom where she dressed and gathered her things.

Her dream man was still asleep; she always had that affect on men. Shaking her head, Trina walked out of the condo and jumped in her cranberry red Jaguar.

As a birthday gift, a boyfriend of hers had taken her car to be detailed. Trina thought it was a cheesy gift, but she went along with it anyway. When he returned the car, Trina noticed something was different, but couldn't put her finger on it.

Trina remembered becoming ecstatic while slowly approaching the car as he opened the passenger's door. The seats of her car were now cream leather and laced in gold trim, with her name embroidered on every headrest. She could've fucked him right there, but she didn't do that for free. Every time Trina sat in the driver's seat, she melted on the soft leather.

Trina pulled out of the driveway. With her mind focused on her job set up for later that evening, she sped through a red light.

The police lights danced behind her car.

"Shit!" she said while pulling over.

The burly, sun-tanned officer exited his car and approached her car. Tina rolled down her window.

"Moving pretty fast, Miss."

"I'm sorry, officer," Trina said. "I guess I have a lot on my mind."

"License, registration, and proof of insurance, please."

*****

When Henson got off the phone with Trina, he put his young secretary to work on relieving his dick.

Damn, just talking to Trina made my shit hard.

As his beef was entertained, Henson replayed the phone conversation in his head. He would have his personal assistant meet Trina at the hotel with the money and room key. *I know it will work out,* he thought while leaning back in his chair and allowing the secretary to perform her magic. After shooting off in her mouth, he waved his hand in the air to dismiss his *special* employee.

All I know is Trina better be as good as Mike said. I'm not paying her all that money for nothing, Henson thought.

Henson was told about Trina over a year ago, but he first saw her outside of a nightclub. She glanced at her diamond-studded watch and then looked around the parking lot. Trina wore a red dress that matched every curve of her body. Her pump's straps wrapped around her ankle and stones that looked like diamonds squeezed her ankle. Henson never knew breasts could be so enticing that they sat up as if God were holding them himself.

Finding himself turned on again, he shook off the memory, stood up, and left the office.

*****

Trina always prepared for her *major* dates by treating herself to the day spa and then a little shopping. After her massage, Trina drove to King Prussia Mall, where it took her three hours to find the perfect little black dress. Trina was all smiles until she saw her estranged stepfather racing towards her. That's when she shoved her hand into her purse and gripped her .38.

"Hey, baby girl. How are you?" Sam tried to embrace her, but Trina backed away.

"Are you serious?"

Sam always acted as if he didn't remember putting his limp dick in her back door without Vaseline. Trina could still hear him whisper, "Oh, I know it feels good." She became nauseated with the flashbacks.

"Back up before I put something up your ass!" Trina yelled, her body shivering as she continued to grip the pistol.

His face dropped, then he turned around and walked out the store.

Shaking with anger, Trina quickly left, hoping to get to her Jaguar safely.

The sound of Mozart rang from Tristen's pocket. He didn't want to answer because it was probably business, and he had promised Shanna a dinner date. When he looked across the table, Shanna stiffened.

"Go on, Tristen. Answer it," she told him.

"I promise it'll be real quick, baby," he said while grabbing the phone from his pocket.

"Hello, it's Tristen."

"Can you hold for the governor?"

"Sure!"

Shanna looked at Tristen because his voice rose an octave.

"Hello, Tristen. I was calling to invite you to have drinks with me tonight at the Hilton downtown. I hope you will accept. Tonight, it'll be about business and then pleasure."

Tristen's face fell. Shanna shifted in her seat.

"Of course, Governor. I'll meet you at the hotel around nine."

"See you then, Tristen."

Tristen hung up the phone. Shanna sat back and crossed her arms.

"Let me guess. You gotta leave me."

"Hey, a meeting with the governor could really boost my ratings. His endorsement could help me win the race. Please understand. I'll make it up to you, I promise," he said, then stood up. "I've got a few more calls to make, so I'm going to step outside for a second. Okay?"

Shanna looked down at her food. "Go the hell on."

Tristen simply bowed his head and left the table.

*****

Dressed, Trina stared at herself in the full-length floor mirror. She studied her face and saw a scared little girl, the same little girl who used to lock herself in the bathroom at night whenever her stepfather got drunk.

I thought I was past it, Trina thought.

Shaking the haunting memories from her mind, she patted her ponytail one last time and then left the condo.

Trina entered the hotel lobby at exactly eight o'clock. She looked around the lobby and spotted an average-looking gentleman. As she walked over to him, he rose from his seat, and when she reached him, he kissed her cheek.

"Ms. Trina, I'm Rick, your host."

Rick was taken aback by her grace. He thought Trina would be the typical whore working in the shadows of Fairmount Park. However, she was the complete opposite.

"Thanks," she said.

They walked to the elevator that took them to the top floor.

"Would you like something to drink?" Rick asked after they entered the suite.

"Not right now. I prefer to handle business first," Trina replied.

Rick pulled out a cheap duffle bag and tossed it on the couch. Trina took her time and counted every last hundred-dollar bill.

"Is everything okay, Ms. Trina?"

"Yes, I'm just recounting to make sure everything is there."

After counting the money, she went to the bedroom, transferred the cash into her overnight bag, and changed into the requested lingerie.

She returned to the living room, where she was greeted with no lights and dancing candles. Food trays sat on the tables laced with cream tablecloths. Wine chilled in a stainless steel ice bucket as soft music played.

"Romantic," Trina said as she walked around the room.

"Okay, Ms. Trina, your guest will be here about nine," Rick told her. "So, be prepared to be extremely entertaining."

Trina smiled. She didn't know if he was trying to come at her, but she didn't respond.

Rick walked toward the door. Then he paused and turned around.

"There's a special gift for you in the bathroom. Go check it out."

When Trina walked to the bathroom, Rick snuck inside the walk-in closet and closed the door. That's where Rick would remain until he had gotten all the pictures he needed of Tristen.

Tristen arrived at the room at nine o'clock and let himself in. He looked confused as he stepped into the candle lit room. Soft music, food, and Trina waited for him.

"Whoa," Tristen said as he stared at Trina. Her beauty consumed him.

Trina walked up to Tristen. His face was unclear in the darkness.

"Hello. Have a glass of wine." She handed him a glass and a robe. Then she kissed him on the neck before walking over to the couch, where she sat down and spread her legs to reveal her secret weapon.

"I think I'm in the wrong ..."

"No, you're not."

Trina stood and grabbed Tristen by his shirt. She led him to the couch and lightly shoved him down onto it. After straddling him, Trina popped every button on his berry-red shirt.

"What's going on?" Tristen whispered.

"You and the friend you brought with you."

When Trina slid her hand to his crotch and massaged his now pulsating manhood, Rick snapped quick, random pictures, hoping to get some good shots.

"No, this can't be going on. Please get up!" Tristen put his hands on Trina's curvaceous ass in an attempt to move her.

Just as Rick was about to snap his final photo of Tristen groping a prostitute, Trina leaned over to kiss Tristen on his neck, blocking Rick's view. Rick was a closet queen, but his nature began to rise at the sight of Trina's flawless body. In a state of confusion, he looked down and watched his dick pulsate like a heartbeat. He was so distracted by his arousal that he didn't notice what happened in the living room.

Tristen stood to his feet and started pacing the floor.

"This must be some kind of joke," Tristen said.

Trina grabbed the robe and wrapped herself in it. Then she crossed her arms.

Tristen took one last look at Trina and walked to the door. *Something ain't right. Let me get outta here,* he thought. *She is too damn fine, and this could get me in trouble.* When he reached the elevator, he called the governor, but got the answering machine. Without leaving a message, he took the elevator down to the lobby and quickly made it to his car.

Trina locked the door and poured herself a glass a wine. *Well, that was an easy twenty grand*, she thought. After dressing, Trina raced to the parking lot to return to the most comfortable and safe spot she knew—her condo.

Overflowing with satisfaction, Rick almost did a cartwheel when Trina made her departure from the suite. He pranced out of the closet and headed straight to the untouched food. With his hands resting on his hips, Rick surveyed the garnished room and decided to partake in the fun before heading to Henson's office.

Chapter 10

The last time Josie spoke to Henson, he claimed to need some time to think. She wanted to reach through the phone and smack the shit out of Henson's old ass. That was two weeks ago.

Josie dressed for work while listening to the morning news. *Idiots! They're amazingly stupid. Seven years in the pen away from family and friends wasn't enough, so the idiots committed a crime every chance that was available,* she thought. Josie shook her head at the 42-inch plasma television that occupied her denim blue-colored bedroom wall. A former inmate, Terrence Ricks, was accused of robbing three sisters that were eighty, eighty-one, and eighty-two years old. However, the sisters whooped his ass with an iron, a bat, and something that resembled a walking stick. The biggest one sat over three hundred pounds of solid fat on his face until the police got there.

"He better hope he doesn't come back to my prison, because I'll have something sweet waiting for his dirty ass," Josie yelled at the television as if the newscasters could hear her.

"Shit, times are hard, but nothing excuses that sort of selfishness," she said as she used the remote to turn off the television.

Josie whistled as she walked down the winding hall and stepped into a junky living room. She kept promising herself that another day wouldn't go by without her tackling the clean-up job. Josie didn't see why she should rush and clean, though. It wasn't like a man frequented her residence.

With her briefcase in one hand and a coffee mug in the other, Josie walked out her front door. Upon reaching her car, she stopped dead in her tracks. Someone scratched the words "WHORE" and "BITCH" on every inch of her car. Josie dropped her coffee and briefcase and examined her car. A wave of nausea hit her.

"What da fuck is going on? I'm going to fuck somebody up! Just wait until I find out who did this shit! Yeah, we'll see who will be the last to laugh, motherfuckers! Motherfuckers!" Josie screamed, while jumping up and down in the street like a crackhead that had lost her last crack valve.

Neighbors gathered in their doorways to get a good look at the ruckus. Everyone was confused about what was going on, but Josie was surely entertaining.

"What da fuck are you looking at? Do you know who did this bitch shit?" Josie hissed at the captain of the neighborhood watch.

Mrs. Baker dashed into her home without a single word. Josie was pissed off to say the least and embarrassed. She did not want to call the police and have them taking pictures of her car that was sure to end up on the front page of *The Daily News*.

Josie was so stunned that she forgot about the midnight blue Lexus that was resting in her garage. When she remembered her second car, Josie began to smile and then fetched her briefcase from the sidewalk. She literally ran to her car and tossed her belongings into the backseat. After slamming the driver's door shut, Josie hit the gas like O.J. should have done when he saw that white girl chasing him.

Josie drove to work in a blur. As soon as she got to her office, she planned to call the police.

"Good morning, Warden. How's everything going?" Samuels asked.

"What? Just buzz me in!" Josie hissed at Samuels.

"Sure, Warden."

Josie wanted to get to her office without being disturbed by the "hello" and "good morning" greetings from the population. She couldn't help but wonder if Henson's wife had anything to do with her misfortune.

Her Nine West boots stomped through the corridor. She made sure her expression matched her walk so no one dared to look her in the face. Sensing her anger, everyone kept their eyes to the floor.

The phone in Josie's office rang like the swat team knocks on doors—persistently. She sat at her desk, looked at the phone, and sighed before answering it.

"Yes."

"Warden, I heard your day isn't going well. However, I need to bring my paperwork to you," Lieutenant Greenwich said.

"Do you have all of my paperwork?"

"Yes!"

"Good. I'll see you in my office in a half an hour. I need to make some phone calls before dealing with this shithole," Josie said.

The warden slammed the phone down in Lieutenant Greenwich's ear. She needed to call the police about her precious pearl vintage Rolls Royce. After the call, she could do inventory of her money.

Lieutenant Greenwich hung up the phone and snickered. He figured the warden was probably having a bad day because of the sensitive information given to Henson's wife about their affair.

"Whatever! It's time for Josie to feel the same heat that she generates for others." He chuckled under his breath. "It's gonna be hard not to laugh in her face," he said to himself, then tossed a paper basketball towards the trash.

Josie heard a knock on her door. She sighed. She hated her job, but she couldn't refuse the perks. The warden looked at the watch that once belonged to her father. She loved that old watch; it was one of the few things that belonged to the man that she never had the pleasure of knowing.

Josie looked up and saw Greenwich standing by the door. He was on time, which was highly unusual. Normally, Greenwich made her wait. *I guess that's how he holds on to his manhood,* she thought.

"Come in," she said.

"Good day, Warden. I have the paperwork you've been looking for." Greenwich stepped into the office and smoothly placed a briefcase on the coffee table.

Josie frowned, a river of wrinkles dawned her forehead. *What the hell is he so happy about?* she thought.

"There's ten grand in small bills in the case."

"Did you count it to make sure?"

"Yeah. How else would I know?" Greenwich replied.

The warden leaned back on the couch and fixed her eyes on the cracking ceiling. She counted the lines while she thought about her exact activities. The lieutenant was her main man, but there were others who helped the operation rotate.

The lieutenant had a few runners that brought the product in the prison from the streets. The messengers dropped the drugs in different vacant parts of the prison for P's and Beast's runners to pick up. After the pickup, they distributed the product amongst their workers. Every other Friday, eight grand was left in a dryer in the laundry room. Another eight grand was placed in a kitchen oven for C.O. Samuels to pick up. The money would be delivered to Greenwich and then to herself to distribute as she saw fit.

Josie wanted to stop playing the game, but she was addicted to the money. She couldn't afford the luxuries in life on a warden's salary.

Rolling her eyes and letting out a huff, she repositioned herself on the couch and looked at the lieutenant with piercing eyes.

"Why are you so, so, so happy? Did you finally get that young girl to give up some ass?" she asked.

"Very funny. I just was enjoying the flowers, sun, and birds. What's your deal today?" Greenwich replied.

"Fool, please get a grip."

Greenwich smiled so hard that his eyes were closed shut and his Chinese neighbors could've mistaken him for kin.

"Josie, what's got your thong too tight?" Greenwich laughed out loud. The thought of Josie in a thong sent shivers up his spine.

"Some asshole scratched obscene words on every inch of my fucking Rolls Royce. That's okay, though. Them jealous-ass bitches didn't stop shit. I simply pulled up in my Lexus."

"Damn, that's fucked up. Who do you think would have the nerve to do some simple shit like that?" Greenwich's hands shook so hard, he dropped the candy dish off the table.

"Why are you shaking like a heroin addict in rehab?"

The lieutenant pretended not to hear Josie as he picked the spilled candy up from off the floor.

"Boy, get your scared ass out my office so I can get to work." Josie walked across the room and opened the door for him to leave.

Greenwich counted his steps to the door. He stopped at Josie's right side and guided the door shut.

"Did you forget about my cut?"

"Nigga, did you forget about the two riots that decreased my profit? You're dismissed!" she said.

"Why are you blaming me for that shit?"

"You can't be that slow. All that happened during your shifts. What happened to supervising?" The warden's face was red as the Kool-Aid man.

"My loss is your cut. Deal with it."

Greenwich stormed out of the office. *One day, I'ma smash that bitch in her face with a two-by-four,* he thought as he walked down the hall.

Before reaching his office, Greenwich ran into C.O. Samuels coming from the ladies' room. He had plenty of steam to blow off. Greenwich smiled at her.

"Samuels, good morning."

"Hi, Lieutenant," she replied.

"Why don't you meet me in the multi-purpose room in about ten minutes?"

"Okay," she said, then thought, *Damn! I wanna say hell no. He just wants a quick fuck, and I'm not in the mood. I know what I'll do. I'll hold a thirty-second conversation with him and then tell him that Paine needs to be relived.*

Samuels walked toward the multi-purpose room, but stopped. *Enough is enough,* she thought. Samuels hurried back down the hall, passing inmates who were cleaning the floors. After directing a few to speed up the process, she continued on her path.

P swept the hall while watching the lieutenant go in the room.

Wonder why that nigga's all angry, P thought as he continued sweeping. *Man, fuck it! He's robbing me blind, wants me to pay too much. Way too much.*

Greenwich had walked passed P without acknowledging him. This bothered P, but the lieutenant didn't mind fucking with that fool.

Fuck, P! I don't understand why so many people are intimidated by the fool, Greenwich thought. Inmates who thought they were running shit always hit Greenwich's funny bone. He guessed that's why they were locked up; the inmates had shit for brains.

Greenwich waited twenty minutes before he realized Samuels had ignored his request. He was foaming at the mouth like a madman diagnosed with rabies.

"Wait 'til I see that whore. She's going to wish she never fucked with me," Greenwich mumbled under his breath as he walked down the hall.

Overhearing Greenwich's rant, P was able to put two and two together. He had seen Samuels standing outside the multi-purpose room and looking inside like the plague was covering the walls. Then almost knocked P down as she scurried away.

They must got some hot shit jumpin' off, he thought. He stopped sweeping and smiled. "Oh shit! Let me find out that nigga likes the blackberry juice," P whispered as he finished sweeping the corridor.

P guessed that since her dude Beast was out of commission, she went on to her next hustle. P wondered about Beast since his recovery had been kept so hushed.

Chapter 11

Samuels called off work for two days after leaving Greenwich to feel himself. When she opened her eyes, dread crept over her. She had to go to work.

How am I going to escape his ass?

She heard her kids running around the house. It was still hard to motivate herself, and her entire house was a mess. She finally found the strength to climb out of bed.

"Let's go! Everyone downstairs now so y'all can eat breakfast! Let's go!"

As she walked downstairs, she kicked debris out of her path. She went to the kitchen and poured cereal for the kids.

The kids ran down the steps like a stampede of elephants. Samuels shook her head while wiping her Italian granite counters. The kitchen was big, so it would probably take her all day to clean it.

After the last child ran from the house to catch the school bus, Samuels heard her phone ring. She followed the ringing to a cabinet. One of her kids came up with the bright idea that the cabinet was a good place for her phone.

"These damn kids are gonna make me catch a case! I swear, I'll call CYS myself and tell them to come get these little fuckers!" Then she yelled into her phone, "Whoever it is, it's too early to be calling me!"

"So you think you're a big girl now."

"What? Who is this?" Samuels asked, although she knew the voice well. It was Greenwich.

"Bitch, you heard me! Did you think I was going to let you off easy for that shit? Did you?" he asked.

"I told you that I don't want to be a part of this shit anymore. I have kids to raise. I can't keep risking jail time for you. Are you going to take care of my children?"

Samuels didn't know where the courage was coming from, but she was feeding off of it.

"Okay, bitch, I got something for you. I bet you didn't know that I work the evening shift tonight, huh?"

Samuels fell from her high rapidly.

She began to cry.

"Greenwich, I'm sorry, but I really can't keep doin' the different things you ask me to."

"Why not? Don't I pay you? I thought money is all that mattered to a whore like you!" he yelled, then hung up.

Samuel screamed to the top of her lungs out of frustration and collapsed to the filthy floor, where she lay on top of the crumbs left by her kids.

What can I do to get this nigga off me? She lay on the floor for a while before it came to her. *Yep, I got his ass.*

Feeling rejuvenated, Samuels crawled to the solid pine chairs and leaned on them to get up off the floor. Using her tongue to play with Greenwich's rusty sack had fucked her knees up. She stood and brushed the crumbs off her, then proceeded to clean the kitchen. She hummed and smiled, confident that her plan would lift the demon off her back. She cleaned until it was time to get ready for work.

*****

After Greenwich hung up the phone, he threw on some old sweats in preparation for his daily jog. He drove to Kelly Drive, where he parked in one of the empty lots. He then exited the Range Rover and stretched. While stretching, his eyes followed the beautiful women jogging down the paths. Greenwich only jogged because of the view.

Greenwich jogged past other runners, walkers, and animal lovers. The river was filled with canoes and young males getting ready for the upcoming season.

I can't believe that witch would undermine me knowing I have her future in my hands, he thought as he jogged along the trail. He paused to take a breath. *I'ma make her lick my ass after a nice long shit. That will teach her who King Kong is.* He chuckled and then proceeded to finish his run.

*****

P lay on his bunk thinking about his future. He needed to find a way to rid himself of a few people and that list included Lieutenant Greenwich, who wanted too much hush money. Greenwich wasn't the one who brought the drugs in, and he didn't push the drugs. So, P found it hard to accept having to give up so much money every other week.

P removed his hands from underneath his pillow and rested his right hand on his johnson. Slowly, he pushed through his browns and Calvin Klein boxers to reach his gift from God.

Just as P started to stroke himself, a low voice said, "You ain't gotta do that."

P didn't have to look up to know who the voice belonged to.

P didn't move as Paine's head floated in the air until landing on his dick. He was amazed at how wide Paine could get her jaws to open before swallowing his piece. Throwing his hands back under the pillow helped P ready himself for the roller coaster ride he knew Paine was capable of giving.

While using her hands and mouth at the same time, Paine sent chills through P. She sucked and twirled her tongue around his fine machinery until she felt a jolt in his body. Refusing to allow P to short her, Paine slid up the bed pole and stood above P outside of his bunk. She dropped her uniform pants to the floor, revealing a smooth, dimple-free ass. Paine wanted P to thrust his dick in and out her ass. Just thinking about it made Paine generate enough juices to drip down her legs.

Knowing exactly what Paine wanted, P stood to his feet with his pants down around his ankles. Smacking the ass one good time always excited Paine, so P cupped his left hand and planted it on her left cheek. Paine let a low moan that fueled P's desire. With caution, P guided his dick in Paine's forbidden spot with no lubricant. His pace picked up at Paine's request. She wanted him to knock her head against the concrete walls that held pictures of Playboy models.

Wanting to receive all the pleasure she could get, Paine used two fingers to quickly massage her clit while

P pounded her ass. Before she knew it, P's hand was over her mouth attempting to muffle her screams.

"Girl, you better be quiet," P whispered in her ear.

Once Paine regained her strength, she straightened her clothes and kissed P goodbye. There was never a disappointing fuck with P.

Paine floated back onto the block, ignoring the stares from jealous inmates who wanted a stab at her ass. Instead, Paine tooted her trunk in the air and switched her behind all the way to the break room.

She opened the fridge to retrieve her lunch, which was leftovers from the night before. After putting her food in the microwave, she turned up the volume on the television. She wanted to hear the latest mayoral debate.

Paine didn't know if she was going to vote for the young bull or the old head. She thought all politicians were career liars, so to her, it really didn't matter who won the election. Shanna, who was in the break room, overheard some of Paine's comments. Shanna's feelings were different from Paine's. She felt Tristen would be the better candidate for the job. He was an honest, hard-working man who wouldn't stop until all his promises were fulfilled.

After watching the debate for ten minutes, Shanna was convinced that Tristen would have victory. She excused herself after grabbing a snack from the vending machine.

Later that day, Shanna passed Paine in the hall. If looks could kill, Shanna would have dried up like an old man's penis. Shanna chuckled and continued past Paine without further thought as she prepared to end her shift. Shanna made it through several exits and finally she was out of the prison.

Shanna noticed Samuels sitting in her beat up Buick in the parking lot as she made her way to her car. The sun had baked the paint job on her car years ago.

Remembering the conversation in the ladies' room at work, Shanna resisted the urge to embrace Samuels, who looked unstable to Shanna.

"I hope Samuels is stronger than her problem," she thought while walking to her car. Shanna backed her Range Rover out of the parking space and exited the lot.

Without noticing Shanna, Samuels opened the driver's door hesitantly and placed her feet on the unleveled ground.

I should just go back home, she thought. *But, if I do, I'll never be rid of him.*

Samuels entered the prison, while thinking, *This must be how inmates on Death Row feel when they take that final stroll.* She went through the security check and headed to her block.

"Glad you could join us today, Samuels. I hope you're over your illness. Clock in and come to my office," Greenwich told her.

"Sure."

Not bothering to do her shift check, Samuels arrived at the lieutenant's office. She knocked on the door ready for whatever punches Greenwich would hurl at her.

"Come in."

Samuels stood in the doorway, leaving the door ajar.

"Close the door and sit down. We may be a while."

Samuels sat down and asked, "What do you want, Greenwich?"

"So you're still feeling froggy, eh?"

"No, I already apologized. What else can I do?" she replied.

"I'm glad you asked that question. For the level of disrespect you displayed, I want you to give me a spa treatment tonight when the kitchen shuts down."

Samuels stood and walked to the door. "Alright, I'll see you then. Is there anything else?"

Since Greenwich didn't respond, Samuels left the office and returned to the block.

Greenwich wasn't sure how to respond to Samuel's reaction to his request. To him, she was a little too quick to agree to his terms. Greenwich rubbed his temples and started his paperwork.

Before going to the block, Samuels stopped at the long-term infirmary. She peeked in to see if the inmate she needed the most was there. Spotting him in the far left corner of the room, Samuels approached him to discuss her situation.

"I really need your help. I know you are in here to recover but I really can't do this any more. I didn't know how to tell you this before, but I'm having serious problems with Greenwich."

"What's the deal, shortie?"

"He has me doing back flips like a trained puppy. I tried to resist that nigga, but he's threatening my job. I can't feed my kids without this gig."

Despite seeing the steam rising off her friend's head, Samuels continued to express her dilemma.

"He got me fucking and sucking whenever he feels an itch. I am working the night shift so if you can help me I will cover for you."

"That bitch must've lost his fuckin' brain cells. Do he know about you and me?"

"Yes. That's what he's holding over me."

As he rotated his head and shoulders, Samuels was reminded of boxers in the ring waiting for the announcer to call their name.

"When's the next time you're supposed to meet up with this fool?"

"Tonight when the kitchen is finishing being cleaned."

"Yeah, keep that appointment. I'm gonna set that white boy straight on some things."

"Thank you. I have to go now. See you later." A grateful Samuels left the infirmary counting down the minutes of the day.

As the evening was winding down, Samuel found it hard to concentrate on her duties. She couldn't stop what was already in motion, so the event was definitely going down.

At last, it was time to meet Samuels in the kitchen. First, Greenwich took a shit. The wetter the dump, the better he felt. Once Greenwich finished shitting, he did a duck walk to the kitchen. To his surprise, Samuels was already there.

She was sitting on the long stainless steel counter, allowing her legs to swing back and forth. For some reason, Samuels seemed really calm to Greenwich. He wanted to see how calm she would be when he dropped his pants.

Adrenaline rushed through Samuels' veins when she walked up to Greenwich. She knew how he liked it, so Samuels dropped to her knees.

"I got a different twist for you tonight," he told her.

"Whatever you desire," she replied.

Greenwich turned around like a trained dancer and pushed his pants down to the cold, freshly mopped floor. Then he bent over so his ass cheeks would spread.

All Samuels could smell was shit. *This nasty nigga wants me to toss his shitty ass.* Samuels became panicky because there was no sign of help.

"Bitch, hurry up. My ass is getting cold."

Before Samuels could lick the lieutenant's butt, she was pushed out of the way. After landing on her right side, she crawled to the nearest corner. Scared to peek from around the corner, Samuels pushed her back against the wall.

"I bet you didn't know this was going to be the last time you were going to pop off, bitch!" Muscular arms quickly wrapped around Greenwich's neck before he could react.

Growing courageous, Samuel jumped up and ran to face Greenwich. She wanted to look him in the eye when his lights were put out.

The inmate revealed a sharp metal object and cut Greenwich's throat like he was gutting a fish.

149

While standing there in shock, Samuels felt a tug on her shoulders. Her savoir was pushing her to leave the kitchen. As Samuels exited the kitchen, she shook to her core.

The show continued. Greenwich was a tough old white ass. He rolled over, bleeding profusely from his neck as he reached his left hand out to the inmate's massive stature. In one swift stomp, his lights were put completely out. Beast stood over Greenwich's lifeless body, beads of sweat forming on his head. He was better, but not fully recovered. His chest heaved up and down quickly. He did not say a word; his pulsating muscles spoke for him. He then staggered from the kitchen without a trace.

It seemed like days went by before Greenwich's body was found. It was near the end of Samuels' shift and still nothing. Samuels almost fainted when she heard the call for the prison to be locked down. The prison was in an uproar once the word got out about

Greenwich. Inmates banged on their cells, while the C.O.'s tried to maintain order.

Samuels felt satisfaction pump through her veins.

*****

The phone's ringing interrupted the best sex the governor ever had. A beautiful, exotic woman rode his dick like a professional horse rider.

"What is it?"

"Are you sure? This shit is going to be plastered all over the news. Try to keep it contained as long as possible."

"Yes I am positive on my way in now!"

The governor pushed his guest off his lap and darted to the next room.

Trina didn't know what the topic of the conversation, but she was thankful for the caller. If she had to stare at the governor's hairy, discolored chest any longer she was going to vomit on him. The governor's hands were clammy, and his breath smelled like old wet rags. Even worse, during the act, his dick had gone down every five minutes until he finally took some Viagra.

"This was wonderful, but it's time to go, hun," the governor told her.

The governor escorted Trina to the front door and then returned to his office to make a few calls. *This shit is going to be a mess,* he thought to himself. The governor opened his desk to find a tablet and was greeted by the envelope that held the pictures taken of Tristen and Trina. The governor couldn't help but think that Trina was worth the money, well worth the money. The pictures were scheduled for delivery to the media.

The governor inhaled deeply and started to make phone calls. In between calls, he tried to rub the pain out of his balls. He didn't know if it was from the superior dick ride or the effects of the Viagra. The morning was off to a bad start. His sack hurt even more when he retrieved his newspaper with "Who

Murdered The Lieutenant?" plastered on the front page. He hadn't seen a scandal of that magnitude in Philadelphia since Wilson Goode and The MOVE people. Backing Henson was becoming a problem.

Chapter 12

While *The Daily News* front page read "Who Murdered The Lieutenant?", the headlines of other papers read "Prisons Don't Offer the Security People Think" and "Killed In the Line of Duty".

Josie cowered in her king-sized bed, laying flat on her back with her brown eyes fixated on the textured ceiling. Her hands were entwined in the crumbled sheets that were draped over the large bed. Josie's pillows were saturated with tears, and her breathing was shallow. Josie's bedroom represented her life—chaotic.

While rolling in the bed, Josie moaned and cried over what felt like the biggest loss of her life. The newspapers drove her crazy. The headlines were giving testimony to the failures that were taking over her life.

"How could Greenwich allow himself to be killed? Why? Why?" she cried.

Because of Greenwich's death, Josie would experience the worse financial drop in history. Although she had a stash her money would be on hold for a while with internal affairs up her ass. She didn't know how the operation would rotate properly without Greenwich. His death not only was outing a turtle in the game, but Internal Affairs would definitely be snooping their hound noses in the prison's affairs. All Josie needed was some goodie-two-shoes to spill their guts, and her ass would be going to federal prison for life.

"Fool! He was a damn fool! What the hell was he doing in the kitchen after hours? Why? Why?" Josie moaned.

As if the news of Greenwich's death wasn't depressing enough, pictures of Tristen Stevens and a whore were plastered across every local news station. This negative publicity would cause Tristen to lose his base; he would plunge in the polls.

What would Henson want with me now? she thought as she rolled over and sat up. *He's going to try and drop me like hot shit. I can't let that happen.*

Josie left the bed and walked to the mirror that dominated the wall closest to the bedroom door. Puffy red eyes stared back at her and made her cry again. Pulling herself from the mirror, she dragged her limp body to the bathroom to wash her face.

*****

"This is Why I'm Hot" blasted from Shanna's cell phone. She looked down at it, knowing another message was sent to her voicemail. Shanna couldn't answer the phone because she had a problem comprehending the pictures of Tristen and Trina. Shanna wiped the tears that flooded her face. At first, Shanna wanted to hunt Trina down and put her size-ten shoe in her nasty ass.

"Stank hoe! Wait 'til I catch that slut!" Shanna threatened the air.

The banging on Shanna's front door snapped her out of her thoughts. Normally, Shanna walked with more grace than a pageant contestant. However, this was not the time for grace. Her stroll matched the stroll of the thugs that she grew up with. Shanna wanted Tristen to be the one on the other side of the door so bad that she could taste it. Behind the beautifully hand carved door was a cast iron bat that Shanna reserved for unwanted guests. After grabbing it, she swung the door open. She planted her feet and lifted the bat, ready to put as much strength in the first swing as possible.

A startled delivery boy stood frozen on Shanna's front steps. His gaze was fixed on the bat that almost cracked his skull.

"I have a delivery for a Ms. Shanna Butler. Is that you?" Without giving her time to answer his question, the red-haired, bright-eyed delivery person stretched a clipboard out to Shanna.

Shanna stepped back into her foyer and propped the bat against the wall. Then she snatched the clipboard from the terrified young man and signed her signature.

"Where's the package?"

"It's not a package, Miss. It's several baskets of fruit and bouquets of flowers. Oh yeah, I have some cards for you, too."

Watching his back, the delivery guy unloaded the items and placed them right inside the doorway.

Shanna didn't ask for the items to be placed further in the house because she figured she had scared the shit out of the boy. Laughing at the nervous guy, Shanna closed her door and went back to her previous thoughts.

Thinking back on past conversations with Trina, Shanna realized she never offered a description of him. Most likely, Trina didn't even know it was Tristen who she had fucked. Therefore, Shanna couldn't be mad at Trina anymore, but she was going to knock Tristen's block off. That nigga didn't have to know Trina, and he damn sure hadn't forgotten Shanna's name. She sat back in the chair and wondered how Trina didn't know how Tristen looked, especially since he was running for mayor! Shanna needed some answers.

Shanna ignored the flowers, fruit, and cards because she was pretty sure Tristen had sent them. She skipped every other step to reach the second floor. After changing into sweats, she left her home. It was time to pay Tristen a visit.

Every phone call Trina made to Shanna's cell phone was sent to voicemail. Trina was one hundred percent sure that Shanna dodged her phone calls. She left messages trying to explain about that evening with Tristen. There's no way Trina would have went if she knew it was Tristen Shanna's man. She could only hope Shanna believed her.

Trina was sitting on a freshly cleaned toilet taking care of business, when the phone rang. The answering machine picked up and her sexy voice soared.

Yes, you have reached Trina, but I am not taking calls right now. Leave a short message…I mean short…and I will return your call soon. Kisses.

Trina held her breath, praying it was Shanna returning her calls.

"Umm, Trina, I'm going to have to cancel for this evening. When the heat dies down, I'll get back with you."

That was the sixth cancellation Trina had received that day. She wasn't really worried about business for two reasons. One, Trina was the best in the business, and two, she had saved enough money to hold her for a few years if she lived a little more sensibly.

Finished with her bathroom break, Trina washed her hands and ran bath water. She had a date with the man who she would have married if he weren't bisexual. Trina caught him bent over the bathroom sink getting plunged in his caramel, baby-smooth ass. The other dude was pumping like he was trying to get oil from a rock. Trina ran back to the living room in search of her gun; she wanted to make both of their asses pulsate. When she got back to the bathroom, the booty bandits were sucking each other off. Trina could still remember the slurping sounds coming from their mouths. Instead of shooting the pair, she eased away from the doorway and let herself out of the apartment. Trina knew her friend wasn't worth catching a case, so she left undetected. Trina never let on how she knew about him.

The bath water was finished and so was Trina's reminiscing. Before soaking her moneymaker, Trina placed another failed call to Shanna.

*****

Shanna arrived at Tristen's office just as Trina's call came through. She wanted to deal with Tristen before speaking to Trina, so she turned her phone off.

When Shanna walked into the office, the workers scattered like roaches when you turn the lights on. She walked towards Tristen's private office just as he opened the door. He stood in the doorway looking like a bum. He seemed to have too many clothes on and a busted pair of Nikes.

"Shanna, nothing happened!"

"What? What are you doin'? Hmm, are you fucking someone in your office right now? And why do you look so shocked?"

"Shanna, it's not what you think. I didn't do anything with that girl. I was set up!"

If Shanna knew anything about Trina, she knew Tristen got a life-size hump in his back from the ride he received from Trina. Shanna rammed the right side of Tristen's face with her iron fist. Then she kicked him in the crotch while picking up the nearest phone to bang his skull in. After damaging Tristen, Shanna strolled out the building to drive off in her car.

*****

Across town behind the walls…

Two Internal Affairs agents waited for Josie to arrive. As soon as she walked through the door, they escorted her to a meeting room where three other agents sat. Josie sat in a black cushion chair that faced her guests.

"Warden Evans, do you know of any inmates who may have wanted to harm the late lieutenant?"

Josie chuckled and responded, "Of course. That would be the entire prison. Greenwich did his job well, so that would have angered just about every inmate in here."

"Okay. Do you know why the lieutenant would have been in the kitchen with his pants to his knees and his trousers full of shit?"

"No. No, I don't," Josie responded with a flat expression.

"Okay, Warden, if we have any further questions, we will be sure to contact you."

Josie walked to her office without looking anyone directly in the face. She wanted everyone to believe she was mourning Greenwich's death. Josie clumsily entered her office without noticing her guest sitting on the red couch. The warden threw her briefcase and jacket to the floor, then sat at her desk. Josie was so startled by the appearance of a woman in her office that she almost pissed on herself.

The sad thing is the prison was a more secure place for the inmates than administration. The warden's office sat on the second floor of the building before you entered the lock-up area with all of the security. Josie's office was just an elevator ride away along with all the other administrators' offices. At that moment, Josie thought lock-up was a better place to be than face to face with a mad woman.

"What the fuck are you doing in here? How did you get in here?"

Mrs. Henson Williams stood about five feet, six inches tall. Her skin was soft and flawless like imported silk, and her hair was pulled into a tight bun. Mrs. Williams tapped her fingers on her black slacks to the same rhythm her right foot was moving. She was pleasantly plump with the thighs of a runner.

Without saying a word, Mrs. Williams pulled a black wood panel from her duffle bag and leaped across the coffee table and desk, landing on Josie's lap. She smacked her across the right side of her face and then the left side. Josie fell to the floor with Henson's wife on her chest and beating her in the face with what felt like an iron ball.

"Help!" Josie screamed.

Officers rushed into the office, peeled Mrs. Williams off Josie, and secured her hands behind her back. Other officers rushed Josie to the infirmary.

Mrs. Williams was placed into a locked room, while the administrator contacted the police and her husband, Mayor Williams.

Samuels walked from the interview room when she saw the warden being hurried to the infirmary. Shaking her head, she kept walking.

She replayed her interrogation in her head. She had way too many other problems to deal with than worrying about the warden. Internal Affairs Officer Christine McKnight grilled her for over three hours. Ms. McKnight was an older woman, with shoulder-length black hair and an attitude that matched her wit. She wouldn't let up on Samuels. She squinted her eyes when she talked, even though she wore glasses. Samuels sat in the chair that felt as if it was mounted over raging hot lava. She squirmed in her seat and tried to focus on other things besides the last time she saw the lieutenant's shitty ass and then his dead, shitty ass. Samuel's emotions were all over the board. She went from being scared and ashamed to infuriated that Greenwich was dead and still controlled her tongue. She leaned back in the hard, black, plastic chair and stared her interrogator directly in the eyes. Finally, Samuels put an end to the dance between them.

Becoming undone, she snarled, "Do you really want to know what goes on in this prison? Just sit back, because this shit is going to sound like a movie script, and the lead character is nothing short of ferocious."

Chapter 13

Screams echoed through the prison like the prey on *Night of the Living Dead*. The inmates on every block felt the crunch of the two-week lockdown. Their cells smelled like livestock was being raised and bred.

"Let me the fuck out of here! This is crazy!"

"This is the shit that happens when inmates think they can cross the line!" an angry C.O. shouted.

The prison was on lockdown for a total of twenty-one days after Lieutenant Greenwich was killed. The inmates were not allowed to shower or come out to use the phone. The smell was rancid on each block. Inmates were threatening suicide just to be let off the block and put on the psych-block where the weirdoes ran free.

Many intelligent inmates who actually had family that cared threatened to get word to the newspapers about the inhumane treatment they were receiving. There were strict laws and policies in the prison that warned against that type of treatment due to the inmates' civil rights and the idea that angry inmates were more likely to start a riot. Despite all of the research and policies, Warden Josie continued to torture the inmates without any relief in sight. She was furious that none of the usual informants she kept on payroll could tell her about the inmate who killed her right-hand man.

P was in his cell going over the math. He calculated all of the money he had lost since the lieutenant was offed. More than that, he was anxious to find out who the hell took out his only source to the crooked-ass warden.

P lay in his soft pillow-top bed trying not to fuel his anger. He had much pull in the place, but the situation the prison was in was cramping his style. His weekly pussy dried up to almost nothing. Paine was not able to make her usual rounds due to the heavy presence of Internal Affairs. P was sick. He had not seen Ms. Butler in a couple of weeks, except when she would peak her head on the block just to be told by the C.O. on duty that no inmate was allowed out of their cell. He reminisced about Ms. Butler's beautiful, substantial ass and instantly smiled.

His light flickered on and off in his cell. P sat straight up and became alert like a soldier at war.

"What the fuck is going on?" he said out loud.

Deep voices giving orders echoed off the walls. C.E.R.T. came onto the block in full force. Niggas scurried to flush their contraband like crackheads scurrying on the street for empty rock vials. C.E.R.T. gave orders and spoke in clear, loud sentences. Every inmate on P's block quivered with fear that they would spend the next thirty days in the hole.

Three big chiseled men with shields and dressed in armor stomped up the steps to the second tier and headed straight for the back of the block. The inmates were speechless. The special agent officers had a specific destination that became more apparent as they passed each cell down the line.

P stood up and looked out of his door.

"Oh shit!" he yelled.

His "untouchable" pass had been revoked. He quickly grabbed a hand full of pepper packets and emptied them on the floor. He was well versed on the drug game. So, he knew he had to confuse the smelling senses of the three dogs on their way to his cell, and pepper was just the remedy for that. P did not have anything in his cell at that moment that could send him up the river, but he knew since more drugs moved through there than the FDA, some residue may have been present. He attempted to flush his camera phone and handheld TV.

"Step away from the toilet!" the officer commanded, then kicked the back of P's head.

The two other officers took residence in the two cells on both sides of him. KM's cell was on his right, and Mont on his left. He closed his eyes and hoped his two soldiers knew what to do in the face of war.

C.O. Samuels had met with Internal Affairs a little over two weeks prior. She was worried they did not buy her story, until she saw her work unravel before her eyes. She stood there in shock as she exited her block on the way to lunch. That's when she saw Rodriguez lead the line of C.E.R.T. to P's block. Rodriguez was a chocolate Latin sex symbol who Samuels used to date before he transferred to the special-ops unit.

Samuels had told Officer McKnight a tall tale that included some important key players that she needed out of the way in order to feel safe again. She told McKnight that P was the trouble in the jail and that he had C.O.'s along with other officials on payroll. She also explained that P and the lieutenant were partners, and that he was the only one to benefit from his death due to a big shipment of drugs and other contraband that was scheduled to be shipped that same night.

"And that is why he was in the kitchen that night," Samuels had said.

Samuels made her story up and included some powerful people. She felt it was the least she could do for Beast after he killed her demon that just wouldn't leave her alone. She figured that with P out of the way, Beast would be the warden's only connect left unscathed. That was a wonderful thought, because it meant more money in her pocket. She knew if she could have a nigga kill for her, getting him to come up off some extra cash wasn't shit.

"After count, all blocks should be released," Warden Evans' voice sounded over the intercom system throughout the prison.

Samuels broke out of her trance. She smiled to herself and thought about how she would put the second part of her plan into play. Since the warden had approved normal movement, Samuels would be able to see her hero without seeming suspicious. She walked through the halls on her way to lunch, preparing the next move she would make to get Beast to come up off that cash.

Greenwich had been an asshole to say the least, but he wasn't a cheap asshole. He paid her well, and now with him gone, somebody had to pick up the slack.

After the count was clear, inmates rushed out of their cells. The block came alive. The inmates fell back into their routines, so one could even tell they were confined for twenty-one days straight. Some cliques convened together as they played spades and had rap ciphers on the side. It was business as usual. The shower line was long due to everyone wanting to get cleaned up.

Samuels made it back from lunch just as the men were being let out. She swung her long, jet-black hair as she put a little bounce in her step. Her body trembled when she saw Beast's sexy, masculine stature. Her thighs misfired as the wetness from her awakened cave seeped through her hot pink thongs.

"What's up, C.O. Samuels?" a fully recovered Beast asked in his sexiest voice.

"Good afternoon to you, too," Samuel replied, fighting back the smile to save face in front of her rookie partner.

"Stay behind the yellow line!" the rookie yelled, while trying to convince himself he wasn't two seconds away from shitting in his pants.

"I apologize, officer," Beast said. "I just need to fill out a maintenance slip. My toilet has been broken for weeks now, and this is the first chance I had since the lockdown."

Handing Beast a yellow slip, Samuels told him to fill it out and return it to the console. Beast's dick throbbed, and Samuels was just the ointment it needed. Beast, who was on restriction from everything, was lucky to be alive. During his long-term stay in the infirmary, he fought hard every day, hoping he would get better to see his love. KM had damaged the base of his neck with two serious stab wounds. The other two wounds were superficial.

Beast knew that once the slip was filled out, one of the officers would have to witness the broken item before maintenance could be called. After Beast completed the slip, Samuels used the perfect opportunity to get in Beast's cell while her partner was occupied by requests from the newly freed inmates.

"I will go check his toilet out while you're handling some other stuff," she said.

"Okay. I'll be fine here."

Samuels followed Beast to his cell, anticipating what she would get when they got to their destination. The inmates were so happy to be out that no one was in earshot of his cell. They both entered like animals, panting and tugging at each other's clothes. They knew they didn't have much time before their absence would be recognized.

Knowing what she wanted, Samuels pulled her uniform pants down to her ankles and braced herself against the chrome sink mounted on the wall. Beast approached her brown, round ass and started kissing all over it. Dropping to his knees, he commenced to lick her split from front to back until her juices dripped from his chin like sweet juice from a ripe watermelon. Samuels moaned slow and sexy to let him know he was giving her what she wanted. Beast could slurp her all day, but he knew time was of the essence. So, he stood up and placed her petite frame on his steel pipe as he inserted his index finger in her asshole. Samuels trembled from a few pumps. Her climax was so good that Beast had to cover her mouth to muffle the screams. He gave her the best ten pumps of his life before sending his soldiers on a journey up her back.

Chapter 14

They say time heals all wounds, but time was not doing anything for this situation. With each passing minute, shit got more complicated. The news must have showed the pictures of Tristen in the hotel with Trina five times per day. With spring passing and summer quickly approaching, time was not a surplus. The people would be making a decision in a few short months about who they wanted as their leader of Philadelphia. Tristen lost some ground, but he still had a lot of people backing him. Shanna all but disappeared from his life and refused all visits and phone calls.

Henson had one up on Tristen for a long four weeks. His polls went soaring once the pictures of Tristen hit the media. He also gained leverage when he fired top prison officials after Lieutenant Greenwich's death. However, his rise in the polls was short-lived. He didn't count on his wife beating Josie.

The warden was hurt, but happy at the same time. Henson's wife had secured Josie's spot in the prison and in Henson's life. Henson did not fire Josie because he still needed her help to get to Tristen.

Henson's wife's charges of assault offset the damage done to Tristen's campaign. Josie was like a trained puppy, and she wanted her master to be pleased with her. She had worked on her plan months before Greenwich was killed.

Josie got out of bed satisfied and excited about what the day would bring. She had finally figured out how she would use the information about Shanna that she had received. This was going to seal the deal and get her man back his rightful spot. Josie checked her outfit for the day. She had a beautiful, soft yellow linen pants suit prepared to adorn her massive body. She accessorized with stark white Kenneth Cole slingback pumps and an oversized white Gucci handbag.

Her insurance paid her well, and she was back in her Rolls Royce. She placed her Gucci shades on and peeled out of her parking spot. Flying up the expressway, she could not wait to get to work to bring this shit to an end. Josie finally pulled into her marked parking spot, arriving a little earlier than she needed to. She wanted to be there before Shanna arrived. She clutched her bag like it was one of a kind and went to her office. When she entered her office, C.O. Samuels was already inside. Josie sat at her desk.

"Good morning, officer. You're quite early."

"When you called and told me to meet you about something important, I hurried here," Samuels said.

"Look, I know I haven't used your services lately, but that was all due to IA up my ass. I have something that's going to make your wait worthwhile."

Josie reached in her top left drawer and took out a tan folder with big red letters that read *CONFIDENTIAL RECORDS*. She handed it to Samuels.

"After you read that, I will explain what I need you to do, and then we can discuss your compensation."

Samuels reluctantly took the file, which contained information on Shanna Butler. Samuels read about how she was caught in a big drug ring and was made to testify at her dead fiancé's trial. Apparently, her previous fiancé was a big kingpin who had been locked up at the prison until a rival drug lord inside the prison killed him. Samuels' mouth fell open as she continued reading page after page of the IA's report. She could not believe the quiet teacher was so hood.

Placing the file on the desk, she asked, "So where do I fit in all this?"

Josie's eyes lit up.

"I'll give you thirty thousand dollars to help me get Ms. Butler for murder and drug trafficking through here," she said.

Samuels looked on. "Continue."

"Well, as you know, I'm good friends with the mayor, and I would like to keep it that way. Her boyfriend is giving my man, excuse me, friend a hard time. This will just up the ante a little bit. Plus, someone has to pay for Greenwich's death. She's the perfect fall guy."

Samuels stared through the warden. She could not believe this ruthless bitch wanted an innocent person set up for her own gain. Josie explained the plan as she reached in her guarded purse to retrieve the package. Samuels reached her left hand out and took the bag as Josie handed her thirty thousand dollars in large bills. Samuels then stood and walked to the staff lockers.

Josie sat impatiently, staring at the clock. Anxiety rushed over her as she waited for Shanna to arrive. She was ecstatic. She could not wait until the plan unfolded to call Henson. She had to let him know what was about to go down. She called, but he didn't answer. Josie hung up in a fit of disgust. She felt foolish that she cared about him so much. She had just handed off a large portion of her life savings and couldn't even get her love on the phone.

Samuels strolled around.

Damn, I came up in a matter of weeks! she thought as she entered the staff's locker room. She opened her locker first and retrieved her cell phone. The voice on the other end did not say much. They just listened intensely to what Samuels had to say. Samuels then went to her assigned area and awaited the call.

Shanna was happy and floating. She was finally getting over the pain and humiliation of the scandal with Tristen. Trina called Shanna, finally getting in touch with her. Trina explained how she had received a strange phone call offering her a large sum of money and how Tristen's name was never mentioned.

Shanna met up with Tristen under the false pretense that she wanted to confirm the story Trina had told her. Shanna's mind was full of make-up sex, and she certainly needed it after a month or more of receiving her sexual pleasure from her bullet sex toy. Shanna arrived at their meeting spot early. She sat in the car with her panties moistening at the thought of Tristen palming her ass.

When Shanna saw Tristen's cranberry BMW pull into the parking lot, she floated from the car and approached him with attitude. Tristen was anxious to see her, but didn't know how their meeting would turn out. The air was warm, but the breeze felt nice on Shanna's bare legs. Tristen was dressed casual in a steel grey linen outfit. Shanna wore a pink, strapless, silk mini-dress with silver jeweled Luca-Luca flats and a matching purse.

"Hello," Shanna said in a dry tone.

"Look, Shanna…"

Tristen was stopped in mid sentence when Shanna planted a soft, wet kiss on him. As their lips touched, both of their bodies trembled. They had held out for almost two months and could not control the hunger for each other. Shanna planned to get and give some off-the-Richter-scale make-up sex. That was why she chose the Drexel Hill Arboretum for their meeting spot. She had a fetish for flowers and Tristen, and having both of them together would result in her having multiple orgasms. Shanna was prepared to recreate a scene out of *Jason's Lyric*, her favorite movie.

Before Tristen could get his thoughts together, they were naked on a bed of lilacs. Shanna moaned and winced with every lick and stroke she received from him. Their light and caramel brown bodies moved as one unit. The smell of sweet flowers and steamy love filled the air as they both released the aroma of forgiveness. Shanna lay next to her soul as the stars bounced off their naked bodies.

*****

Shanna entered the prison with thoughts of her wonderful evening with Tristen on her mind. Suddenly, her euphoric feeling was interrupted when she was surrounded and escorted to the captain's office. Shanna's eyes grew wide, and she questioned the reason for the dramatic entrance. Once she was placed in the office, the new lieutenant ordered her to tell who she was smuggling in drugs for.

Samuels heard the call for her over the intercom. She knew what that meant. Showtime!

By the time she arrived in the captain's office, she saw that one of her fellow officers was already present. Samuels had to think quickly on her feet if the plan was going to work. She knew all of Ms. Butler's belongings and her locker and vehicle were subject to search, so she began to delegate quickly.

"Captain, I will strip search Ms. Butler, and Officer Jones can search her locker with the K-9 unit."

"Good thinking, Samuels. I will give the order."

Samuels escorted Shanna to the warden's office where the strip search would be private. Warden Josie exited her office and stood guard at the door as Samuels pretended to follow procedure. Shanna shook while tears flowed down her face like streaming rivers of sorrow. The humiliation reminded her of her late fiancé's trial and how she had been pulled into something she wasn't even involved in. Each piece of clothing shed was a piece of her dignity.

Shanna was clean. Josie fought back the joy. She knew the search of her locker would reveal the drugs to the captain, with the help of the K-9 unit.

Samuels escorted Shanna out of the warden's office and down a long stairwell. Co-workers stared at her as if she was taking the walk of shame. Their eyes felt like millions of fingers violating her. Shanna was confused about the route that C.O. Samuels chose to take back to the captain's office.

Twenty minutes passed, and the warden restrained from celebrating. As she picked up the phone to call Henson again, there was a tap at her door. She was sure it was Samuels coming to tell her the good news. When the door flung open, there stood Officer McKnight accompanied by two other officers.

"Good morning, Ms. McKnight."

"I don't know how good your morning will be, Warden."

"What brings you by here this morning without a phone call?"

"We don't call people that we come to search and interview."

The warden chuckled at the officer's tone. "What are you saying, Officer McKnight?"

"What I'm saying is that I need you to step away from your desk and stand with the two gentlemen behind me. I will be searching your office, and depending on the outcome of the search, you will be questioned here or at the police precinct."

Josie stood and stepped away from the desk. "You're gonna owe me an apology after this!" she snapped.

Officer McKnight walked straight to her desk and began her search. When she came across Josie's locked drawer, she asked her for the key.

Josie responded, "There's nothing in there except a gorgeous Gucci bag. Maybe you'll like it."

Officer McKnight searched her drawer and then slowly removed all of the contents of her purse. A hairbrush, floss, and spare keys were among the items found in her bag. Officer McKnight's face displayed wrinkles everywhere; she had trouble getting a small bag from the very bottom of the bag. She grasped it and pulled out a brown bag wrapped with duct tape.

Josie's breathing sped up, and she began to drip sweat like a fat WWF wrestler. The exact bag she had given Officer Samuels to place in Shanna's locker had reappeared like Jason Voorhees.

As Officer McKnight questioned her about the bag, Josie stood paralyzed with tears streaming down her face. Her life, career, and most of all, her precious lover was gone…and so was she.

The End

Shanna was speechless as she read the last words of Josie's book. Attached to the manuscript were tapes, pictures, and a handwritten letter addressed to Josie from Samuels, which read:

Josie Evens, PP#579887
Muncie State Corrections, Muncie, PA.

Dear Josie,
Thank you for being the greedy, self-centered, obsessed bitch you are. I am enjoying my new position, and my day-to-day business is booming! Your partner was a lousy lay, but his money sure keeps me warm at night. My only regret is playing the scared, stupid horse to you two imbeciles, when in

actuality, the horse was the stable owner. Thanks for making me rich,
BITCH!

Signed,
Your Boss aka Warden Samuel

P.S. BEHIND THESE WALLS EVERYTHING IS NEVER WHAT IT SEEMS. IT'S JUST A MIRAGE. THE PIMPS GET PIMPED, TOO…